POSITIVES & PENALTIES

A Slapshot Novel

HEATHER C. MYERS

Chapter 1

EMMA WINSOR STARED at the white plastic stick, her brown eyes wide, her face pale. How was it possible that two parallel pink lines could completely change her life?

She leaned her head against the bathroom wall, her legs curled underneath her. She refused to touch the stick. Refused to make it real to her. She closed her eyes, thinking back to when this could have possibly happened. She was always so careful. He was always so careful. When they were in Vegas, they messed around, got tipsy, and now, she couldn't remember if Kyle had actually used a condom or if they said fuck it.

She shook her head.

This was not her. She was careful. She planned for things. She always made sure her actions were reflections of carefully crafted choices that would help her future, that would assist her in reaching her goals that she wanted since she was a child.

She closed her eyes, slowly exhaling through her nose. She was on the edge of the closed toilet seat, in her adjacent bathroom. Her father was still at work but they would be meeting at the Sea Side Ice Palace due to the fact that tonight was the game clincher that decided whether or not they were guaranteed the fourth seed in the Pacific Division. It was an incredibly important game. Afterward, she planned to go out with Kyle and the rest of the team to celebrate because naturally, the team expected to make playoffs and the fourth seed would be amazing. It meant they would be playing Las Vegas and that, by itself, would make an excellent first series.

Plus, the team would make history. The Newport Beach Seagulls had yet to make a playoff run in the entirety of the twenty years that they'd been an official national hockey team. They had been a mediocre team, started by Ken Brown, a native Californian with a passionate love for hockey even though he never played it. He was a billionaire and took losses the first seven years the team was part of the NHL. But then he started drafting young talent, started acquiring trades worthy of an established franchise. The team became a challenge to beat. It was a team that got into a lot of scrums. They never made playoffs while Ken was alive but dammit if they didn't make the other teams work.

And then, one day, Ken was murdered by his accountant. Seraphina Hanson, his youngest granddaughter, inherited the team. And that year, they absolutely were terrible. Seraphina knew nothing about the business of hockey.

But she learned.

And she started making some noteworthy trades. She managed to acquire Zachary Ryan, James Negan, and veteran defenseman, Duncan Jackman. She picked up some young kids in the past draft that were doing well in the minor league team, located out of Irvine. She did have a couple of misfires - like bringing Matt Peterson back after he demanded to be traded after Ken's murder (he also happened to be dating Katella Hanson, Seraphina older sister at the time), but Matt was a solid third-line center. So, Emma supposed, it seemed to work out. For now.

And this year, the team was outstanding. More Canadian news channels gave them time on air rather than dismiss them as nothing but a bunch of goons - or worse - ignore them completely. But the Gulls forced them to talk about the team. And after tonight, they'll be part of playoffs and have earned their stripes, so to speak.

A thousand thoughts swam through her head, each one more fire than the last. Her dreams were gone. She didn't realize how quickly dreams could simply disappear before her very eyes. It was as though she had blinked and they were gone. That was how bad it was.

Tears blurred her vision but she blinked them away. Emma refused to allow herself to play the victim. She was a willing participant in the sexual activity that had produced the growing child inside of her. She wasn't allowed to feel sorry for herself. What she needed to do now was weigh her options.

First, she could keep it. She had money and she knew that her father would support her, even if he was disappointed in her decision-making - which he had every right to be. Secondly, she could carry the child to term and then give the child up for adoption. This seemed like the last option she would ever consider due to the fact that she knew what it felt like being abandoned by her mother and there was no way she was planning on doing that to her own child. Her last option was to get an abortion and while she was always pro-women should be allowed to do whatever the hell they wanted with their bodies, she wasn't sure why her personal feelings were now that getting pregnant accidentally had happened to her.

She had two extremes to pick from. Her head was swimming with choices and it was too overwhelming for her to stop and consider this rationally.

But she didn't have to decide right now. And maybe she should talk to Kyle about this before any of the decisions were actually made. He was the father, after all, and even though the decision ultimately rested with her, she felt it was only fair to give him some kind of head's up about the situation.

Maybe serious discussion was the more apt phrase for a matter such as this one.

She groaned. She couldn't even imagine having this conversation with Kyle just yet. He already had enough on his plate - making playoffs, playing a good game. Despite the fact that they were serious about each other, Emma knew he wasn't ready to get married and have children just yet. Not when there was always that possibility he could be traded - she nearly snorted at this thought; not likely, considering what an asset he was to the team. Not when he was still young and wanted to go out after wins to celebrate with the guys rather than come home to a crying baby.

And what about her? New York was a distant memory. She wouldn't be able to work as hard when she got into her second and third trimesters. Her entire career had to be put on hold so she could have this baby.

How had this happened?

It had to have been in Vegas a few weeks ago. She had gotten to the hotel late. They had all gone out. They had gotten tipsy.

Emma never drank but she had also never been to Vegas and she wanted to experience it the way she should - with the man of her dreams, completely drunk. And honestly, it was one of the best nights of her life. She had fun with Kyle. She loved being wrapped up in him, smelling his musky aftershave mixed in with a masculine hint of his sweat. Loved watching those crystal blue eyes turn dark as his desire for her wrote itself on his face. Loved the way his tongue teased every inch of her skin.

She shivered just thinking about it.

However, Emma was certain he had a condom that night. He had to. He was just as careful as she was, if not more so.

It wasn't as though he wanted to be a young unwed father. He was still in the prime of his life, having his fun with his friends. The fact that he settled down and was in a serious monogamous relationship with her was a big deal.

So either she totally forgot that they didn't have a condom or they did have a condom and it was somehow defective. Because regardless of what did or didn't happen between them that night, she was pregnant. Although... maybe she should take a second test just to be sure. She furrowed her brow. Wasn't it more common to get a false negative than a false positive? And it wasn't like she was squinting, trying to decipher if the second line was an evaporation line or a legitimate line. It was pink and bold, staring at her with mocking certainty from the little window. There was no denying that this test was positive.

She huffed a sigh. She needed to talk to someone about this. Someone she could trust. Someone who wasn't her father and wasn't Kyle. Seraphina and Katella were probably too busy, what with the team probably making playoffs. Emma reached up and grabbed her cell phone, currently sitting on the counter if the bathroom sink.

She quickly unlocked and dialed her only other friend she wanted to share this with. Harper Crawford.

———

HARPER SHOWED up fifteen minutes later with sandwiches from C'est Si Bon, a sandwich place on PCH.

"I got you egg salad," she told Emma after Emma showed her in and the two walked to the kitchen. "You're not supposed to eat deli meats. And fish. And if you can cut out caffeine, that's awesome, but if not, cut back."

Emma shot Harper a look. "How do you know all of these things?" She murmured, taking a seat at the bar island, across from Harper as she started passing out the sandwiches.

"I read a lot," she replied. "Zach and I are talking about having kids. Eventually."

Emma shot her friend a look consisting of narrowed, suspicious eyes and lips pressed tightly together. "Are you serious?"

she asked. She hadn't meant to sound so judgmental but she couldn't take the words back once they were out in the open.

"I wouldn't joke about something as serious as kids, Emma," Harper told her and Emma felt rightly reprimanded. "Zach and I talk about everything. We're planning to spend the rest of our lives together so of course we would talk about kids and that sort of thing. We want three, in case you were wondering."

"But you're my age," Emma said, still confused. Still flabbergasted. "How can you know Zach is the one when you haven't even been dating a year?"

"I knew a month into it," she said. "And he knew even sooner than that." She shrugged her shoulders and took a bite out of her tuna melt. "The thing is, when you know, you know. And that's not something to be scared of." She cocked her head to the side. "Are you doubting Kyle's feelings for you?"

"This has nothing to do with Kyle's feelings and everything to do with mine," Emma said. She hadn't even touched her food, even though it was her favorite type of sandwich.

Harper cut her a look that told Emma she didn't believe her. "Okay," she said, relenting. "Tell me about your feelings then." Emma stared blankly back at her friend and Harper grunted with impatience. "Come on, Emma. What do you feel? It's not that hard!"

"I feel fucking terrified!" she exclaimed, throwing her hands up. The swear word was foreign in her mouth and she couldn't look at Harper as she said it. But Harper wanted the truth and Emma was going to give that to her. Emma was going to give it to herself. "I have no idea what I'm going to do, Harper. I have no idea if I want to keep it. My dreams of New York and Broadway are gone. They're gone all within the three minutes it took for the stupid second line to appear. I have no idea how Kyle is going to respond to this. We haven't even talked about kids yet, Harper, let alone marriage. I'm so lost and confused and scared."

Harper took Emma's rant in silently, her lips pressed

together. She picked her eyes up from her sandwich so she could look at Emma, trying to figure out what she should say and how she should say it.

"Em," Harper said slowly. "Do you know if you ever want kids?"

Emma opened her mouth to respond before closing it and cocking her head to the side. "You mean, like in the future?" she asked slowly.

Harper nodded. "Yeah," she said. "Do you know if you want kids in the future at any point in your life?"

Emma was silent for another moment. "Honestly," she began but then paused and shook her head. "Honestly, I've never really thought about that part of my future. I know what I want out of my life, career-wise, but I never really thought about having kids or getting married."

Harper pressed her brows together and tilted her head to the left. "Why?" she asked. "You're in a serious relationship with a man. You've been together for over a year. Don't you care about where your relationship is going?"

Emma clenched her jaw. "I never really thought about it," she admitted, her voice still coming out defensive. "I just always assumed..."

"That Kyle would be there," Harper finished, her voice quiet as she looked at her friend with an intense stare. "Let me ask you: I know you applied to all of these places in New York to go to school for dance. I know your dream is to dance in Broadway. Does Kyle know these things?"

"He knows I love dancing," Emma told her but Harper shot her a look that interrupted her. "Okay, no, I don't think I've ever told him these things."

"Why not?" Harper asked.

"Because he's focused on his dreams, I'm focused on mine," Emma replied, running her fingers through her hair and dropping her eyes down to her sandwich. "I don't want to bombard him with my issues when he has his own issues he has to worry about."

"Emma, that's what partners do for each other," Harper said as though it was the most obvious thing in the world. "You're there for each other. You notice when something is wrong and ask. You talk about your dreams and your goals and you figure out how to incorporate each other so his dreams are yours and vice versa." She pressed her lips together. "Okay, well, I gotta go get ready for tonight. Emma, I'm here for you always. I'm not going to tell you what to do. But consider figuring out what you want out of your future with Kyle. I think you guys could be even better together than you already are."

She squeezed Emma's shoulder before seeing herself out, leaving Emma alone in her kitchen with a delicious egg salad sandwich she couldn't bring herself to eat.

Chapter 2

EMMA WAS NERVOUS. She had no idea why she was nervous - she never got nervous before a game. Typically, she tried to keep a cool head so Kyle wouldn't see her nervous. She needed to be the strong one so he could focus on the sport, on his game, and not worry about pleasing her. But tonight, sitting next to her father as she stared out of the recently-washed glass, watching both teams warm up on their respective sides of the ice, she felt her stomach twist into knots beyond her control.

There was a good chance her nervousness was primarily regarding her new pregnancy rather than this particular game and it was manifesting itself now. She had no idea what to tell Kyle. Hell, she had no idea what to tell her friends and her father. She had no idea what to tell her dance students at the studio she worked at. She had no idea what to tell the dance academies in New York, where she applied to attend so she could live out her dream and dance on Broadway.

She clenched her jaw. She didn't want to think about that. There was no way she'd be able to attend even her last choice. No one was going to accept a pregnant woman. There was no way.

"You okay?"

She nearly jumped at her father's question, even though the stadium was already noisy with mainstream music playing and fans cheering their favorite players. She forced a smile on her face she knew her father would be able to see through so she didn't even bother lying.

"Nervous," she admitted.

He took her hand, a small, knowing smile on his face. "They've got this," he assured her.

Emma curled her fingers around her father's hand but didn't respond. Instead, she focused her attention on Kyle. He was always so intense before a game, so focused, he never looked for her in the crowd. Which was fine. He knew she was there and that was all that mattered. She completely understood. Hell, she was the same way with dance. But, for some reason, she really would have wanted him to look up from his stretching and give her that crooked smile reserved just for her. Which was selfish.

Tonight was about him, not about her. She shouldn't expect him to reassure her when he was fighting to make history. She could handle this lump of emotions. She had to.

The game started just after the national anthem. Emma leaned forward, her elbows resting on her knees. It was Negan's line that started - James Negan was a veteran second-line center currently dating Seraphina's older sister, Katella - and he had Drew Stefano and Viktor Jansson as his wingers.

They were playing their cross-town rivals, the Hollywood Stars. They had already guaranteed themselves the first seed in the Pacific Division so they might not be playing as hard as usual in order to ensure none of their players got injured unnecessarily. However, if Emma knew the Hollywood Stars, and she had a feeling she did, she had a feeling they would go out of their way in order to attempt to ensure the Gulls lost this game to make acquiring even the wildcard seed of the division that more difficult. She expected a gritty game.

"You hungry?" her father asked her, leaning back in the plastic navy blue chair, tilting his head to stare at her profile.

Was it possible to notice pregnancy just by looking at her face?

There was no way, right?

"Um..." She pressed her brows together, unsure. Was she hungry? She hadn't thought about food since she found out she was pregnant, truth be told, and she wasn't sure how she felt about food now.

To be honest, she hadn't experienced any pregnancy symptoms. In fact, the only reason she had taken a pregnancy test in the first place was because her period was four days late and it was never four days late. Even then, she was going over her routines and her diet, making sure she wasn't exercising too much and eating too little. Pregnancy was the last thing on her mind.

Until it was her only explanation.

"Yeah," she finally said, locking eyes with her father. She needed to appear as normal as she could be without raising suspicion. "Yeah, I'll take some chicken fingers."

Emma had always been picky with the quality of her food. She didn't drink soda and rarely indulged in sweets. Her only exception was when she was at a hockey game. When she was here, she allowed herself to indulge in fried foods, sugar, and junk food. Every now and then, she would request a healthier option - fruit, chicken wraps - but her favorite was chicken tenders or unsalted pretzels with tons of nacho cheese on the side.

If she didn't want her father suspecting anything, she needed to act like she normally would, which meant ordering what she normally did.

"And a bottle of water," she said.

"Chocolate?" he asked, standing up and tilting his head to the side.

She grinned. "Kit Kat, please," she said.

He nodded. "Be right back," he said and headed up the steep stairs.

She let out a shaky breath. That wasn't so bad. She could do this. She could totally avoid telling her father about this.

Actually, no she couldn't.

Emma had managed to avoid him thus far. Considering they were at a hockey game, it was the perfect distraction for him not to pick up on how incredibly awkward she felt around him. But he would. Her father was a lawyer after all, and more than that, he knew her well enough to know when she was lying and when she was hiding something. Plus, she couldn't lie to save her life. Hell, if he looked at her straight in the face and asked if she was okay, there was no way in hell she'd even be able to respond.

Because she couldn't lie.

Which meant she needed to figure out how the hell she was going to handle talking to him about this because if she couldn't lie and couldn't hide this from him, she would have to tell him.

But do I tell him before I tell Kyle? she thought to herself. I don't know the proper protocol when it comes to this stuff. I've never been pregnant before.

'There isn't a proper protocol,' a voice that sounded suspiciously like Harper's pointed out. 'This is part of being a parent. You figure it out. And it's hard, yeah. But it'll be okay in the end. It'll all work out.'

Emma scrunched up her nose. Sometimes, Harper's bubbly positivity made her want to pop a balloon. It was easier being on the outside looking in. Nobody knew exactly how she was feeling. Nobody could make the right decision for her except her. Because she was experiencing it.

She just needed to figure out what the best decision was for us.

"Hey," her father said, seemingly coming out of nowhere and taking his seat beside her. He handed her food and water. "You okay? You seem pensive."

Emma nodded, forcing a smile that she knew was too bright

into her face. "Just going over steps for the spring recital," she told him.

He nodded, momentarily appeased.

It wasn't long before the lights went down and the announcer introduced the Newport Beach Seagulls. Emma got goosebumps as she typically did at the start of the game. She forgot for a moment that she had this huge elephant on her shoulder, and instead, leaned back in her seat and focused on her boyfriend.

Emma could see him clearly since their seats were just behind the Gulls' bench.

He wasn't typically good looking but he was tall and built, and when he smiled - which was rare, especially on the ice - his entire face lit up and his crystal blue eyes sparkled, which took her breath away. He had blond hair and pale skin - growing up in Regina, Canada, was a cold experience, from what he told her - and a sharp jaw. Regardless of what was deemed typically handsome in this society didn't mean she believed the hype. Each time she looked at Kyle, remembered how dark his eyes would get as they looked at her, how his callused palms felt against her most sensitive skin, she shivered and felt her thighs moisten.

'See, this is how you got yourself into this mess,' a voice pointed out. 'You're crazy about him.'

Emma felt her lips curl up. "So what if I am?" she muttered under her breath. "There's nothing wrong with that." And despite what had happened, her feelings hadn't changed.

Currently, Kyle was stretching across the ice, down on his knees on the ice. The groin muscle was extremely important in hockey and one of the muscles that was easily pulled during a game, especially for the goalies. Kyle was one of the few players who actually stretched on ice on top of skating and shooting during the warm ups. He never wore his helmet, which made no sense to Emma since he could get hurt, even during warm ups, but at least he got to see his face clearly, and at least he did choose to wear a shield.

Shields offered protection against flying pucks and sticks. The NHL was now enforcing that all new players wear a shield despite their preference, though older players did not have to, including Zachary Ryan and Dean Morgan, one of the veteran defensemen that was tough as nails and just an asshole both on and off the ice.

Emma pressed her lips together, taking in the sight of her boyfriend, the conversation she had had with Harper coming back to her. She loved being with Kyle. She loved being intimate him and talking to him and watching Netflix on his time off. During the hockey season, she pulled back because she thought he needed space and he hadn't told her otherwise. Plus, she had dance to focus on.

But maybe, maybe Harper was right. Maybe they needed to take their relationship to a deeper level where they talked about the future and where they expected their relationship to go.

Was that what she wanted?

The more she stared at him, the more she realized that yes, she did want that. More than she realized.

Chapter 3

THERE WAS a tornado of emotions swirling in Emma's body as the final buzzer sounded and the Gulls won the game. They were officially going to the playoffs for the first time in their history. The entire team skated towards Brandon Thorpe, their starting goalie, and tackled him to the ground in a fit of uncharacteristic uncontrolled emotion.

Emma jumped up and down, pounding on the glass in front of her, cheering her heart out. The unexpected turn her life was taken was momentarily forgotten. She let happiness sweep her up into a blissful state of ignorance as she watched Kyle, Alec, and Zachary all throw their gloves up in the air and hug. Drew Stefano jumped into the glass, his body bouncing off as the nearby crowd pounded on the glass, celebrating with him. The two older defensemen - Jackman and Morgan - had smirks on their faces, their eyes revealing their excitement more so than their gestures.

After another moment of celebration, the players grabbed their sticks and held them up. Following Thorpe, they skated up and down the ice, waving their sticks at the crowd, as though to say 'thank you.'

Kyle's eyes found her in the crowd and he gave her that crooked smile that made her heart skip a beat. All of her doubts, all of her worries, simply vanished.

Things were going to be okay. Everything was going to be okay.

"What are you guys doing tonight to celebrate?" her father asked her, tilting his head down so he could whisper in her ear.

"Probably Taboo," Emma replied. "It's a team favorite."

It wasn't long before the crowd filtered out. After kissing her father on the cheek, Emma slid into her seat, waving at Madison Montgomery, one of the Gulls' Ice girls who cleaned up the ice during commercial breaks and provided fun entertainment such as shooting t-shirts into the crowd. They were also known to rally the crowds, trying to garner enthusiasm and loud cheers. They also assisted with the various charity events throughout the year.

Madison and Emma had gotten close simply because Emma had been dragged along to a variety of charity events with her father and didn't have anyone to really talk to before she officially started dating Kyle. There were rumors she was dating a player but Madison hadn't said anything to Emma, and quite frankly, Emma didn't think it was anyone's business anyway, regardless of whether it went against policy or not. And she wasn't going to push and ask who it was, even though she was curious.

Madison gave her a grin and waved back, skating off the ice with her fellow Gulls Girl, Amanda.

When she was left by herself - save for the ushers who began cleaning everything right away - she let out a breath. Her thoughts turned back to her stomach - rather, what was in her stomach. She hadn't even attempted to figure out her due date but now that she had time to kill, why not?

She grabbed her phone and went to the first website that offered to calculate it based off the first date of her last menstrual cycle.

She had always been pretty good at keeping track of that just because she wanted to know so she could schedule her classes around it, if she could. Not that it was so bad she didn't want to work through it but she would rather curl up with a good book in front of her fireplace and fall asleep on the couch, listening to the flames cackle into the night. She loved to be alone when she was on her period because she tended to get aggravated easily and she didn't want to snap or take it out on anyone. Especially not Kyle. Especially not her father.

Both men seemed okay with this, even though they wanted to be there for her if she ever needed them to be. Emma had always been independent and just because she was in a serious relationship with Kyle wouldn't change that all that much. Though there were times she relished in the fact that if something happened at one of her classes or one of her friends was being a bitch, she could call him and vent. And since dating Kyle, Vince had stayed away for the most part, which was a welcome relief.

She typed in the date - February 2. She remembered because they were already planning Vegas and she was ecstatic that by the time they were over there, she would most definitely not be on her period anymore. On top of that, she didn't have to worry about Valentine's Day considering she would be ready to go at that point.

November 9.

Currently, she was five weeks pregnant.

She let out a shaky breath. This made it real. She had an estimated due date of when this baby was supposed to arrive. Considering it was the middle of March, she had a lot of time to prepare.

If she was planning on keeping it.

She clicked her phone off and leaned back in the chair, her eyes looking at the fresh ice. The Zamboni had just cleaned it and now it glistened under the lights. She still had a few minutes before she would head out and walk to her car. There was something so peaceful about being the only person in a hockey stadium, staring at a fresh sheet of ice. If she spoke, her voice would echo through the building. The lack of people made it even colder. She smiled. Despite the turmoil she was currently facing, it was nice to be somewhere calm, where she could forget her problems for a little while.

"You almost ready to head out?" a friendly voice asked.

Emma turned her head and smiled at her favorite usher, an older gentleman named Steve. He was average size, with greyting hair and glasses. He was retired, portly, and soft-spoken. The perfect person to have a hockey conversation with since he was originally from Canada and was actually a Vancouver Grizzlies team.

She nodded and pushed herself into a standing position. She would meet Kyle in the locker room, which she was allowed to head towards once the stadium was clear and the press was gone. She took the elevator down and upon recognizing her, the secretary waved her through, past her desk, down a long cemented hallway that housed both locker rooms, plus a smaller one specifically reserved for the Gulls Girls.

There was a bench outside the home locker room, and Emma took a seat on the leather cushions, waiting for Kyle to emerge. Normally, Harper would already be here due to the fact that she was technically press and was actually given first dibs on interviewing players because she was their official blogger. However, she wasn't there and Emma wondered if she and Zachary had already left. And if that were the case, did that mean the group was still going out like they planned?

Or maybe Harper insisted they leave early so Emma and Kyle could be alone. Which would be just like her. The problem was, Emma didn't know when to tell Kyle, how to tell Kyle, where to tell him. And she wanted to make sure she took care when telling him because this was a big deal and she didn't want to scare him off.

Because what if he left her as a result of this?

Emma clenched her teeth together and looked away. She hadn't allowed herself to really think about this but she also couldn't deny it, either. She might claim she was only thinking about herself right now, rather than about how Kyle was going to react, but the truth of the matter was, she was afraid. She didn't know if he would be happy or if he wouldn't want anything to do with her. They were happy together and they did make plans - this summer, he wanted to bring her back to his place in Regina so she could meet his parents - but they had never talked about marriage and kids.

Should they have?

They had been together for nearly two years now. That was a serious-type of relationship for both of them. It hadn't even crossed her mind, however, to think about marriage and babies just yet. She was just a year out of college. She didn't think she was ready to be a missus, to be a mom, just yet.

Why do you assume that having a child automatically means getting married? a voice asked. *Because it doesn't. People have babies out of wedlock all the time. It's not even a big deal anymore.*

That was true. But what if he tried to do the right thing - supposedly - and proposed just because she was pregnant? She didn't know if she wanted to be married to the guy. She did know she loved him. She knew she didn't want to be with anyone else.

But marriage?

Emma sighed. She seemed to be doing that a lot lately.

"Hey Emma!" a familiar voice shouted.

Emma turned and found Madison Montgomery emerging from the Gulls' Girls locker room in a pair of boyfriend jeans and a long-sleeved shirt with nautical styled stripes. She had a Gulls cap over her dark, wavy hair, which billowed around her as she walked over to her friend.

"Hey Madison," Emma said with a smile. "Great job tonight!"

Madison grinned. "Thanks," she replied. "It feels good actually being on the ice rather than being in the crowd. Not that I don't appreciate the whistles and the ass-grabbing, it's just nice to take a break from it all." Her blue eyes glanced around before resting in Emma's once more, a curious look on her face. "Where's Kyle?"

"Probably taking a shower," Emma replied with a shrug. "We didn't really get a chance to talk before the game so he might not realize I'm waiting for him."

Madison wiggled her eyebrows. "Or he's waiting for you to go in there," she replied. "I think everybody else left so if Kyle is still in there, he might be the only one." She smirked and Emma laughed.

"And what about you?" Emma shot back. "When am I going to meet this mysterious boyfriend of yours?"

Madison chuckled. "I have no idea what you're talking about," she said but even she couldn't stop the pink blush from gracing her high cheeks. "I'm graduating this year so I need to focus on that. I only have a couple of months before graduation."

"Sure, sure," Emma said, rolling her eyes. "Have a good night!"

Madison waved back. "I am serious, you know," she said, turning around so she could keep eye contact with Emma but continued to walk. "All the players are gone. I would check up on Kyle. He may have a surprise for you. You never know." With one last wink, Madison spun around - nearly running into a cardboard cutout of Alec Schumacher - and headed for the elevators that would take her to the main floor and to the parking lot.

Emma shook her head and glanced back at the locker room. If there was no one else there, it couldn't hurt to make sure Kyle was okay. He had a rough game - two guys, two penalties, and no points. In fact, the Stars had scored while he was on the ice so he was a negative one for the game.

Emma had noticed he wasn't playing as well as he could

have been. She wasn't sure when it started but it had to be within the last few weeks. She hadn't thought to ask him why because she figured he would have told her himself at some point, when he was ready to share that information.

She was so stupid, she realized.

Kyle was just as guarded as she was. He wasn't going to go out of his way to tell her anything if she didn't notice that on her own.

She took in a breath and stood up.

At least she knew what she needed to work on. At least she could start making things right, at least on her end.

Because she did want him. She wanted to be with him. And maybe they could figure out the next step out together.

Chapter 4

EMMA TENTATIVELY WALKED over to the locker room. She wasn't sure if she was supposed to knock or simply go in. She did know she didn't want to walk in on any naked players who weren't her boyfriend so she knocked a few times before placing her ear on the door.

Nothing.

No sound. No movement. Simply... nothing.

She huffed a breath and opened the door slowly, waiting for anyone to shout out that they were changing or to close it but nobody did. Instead, she found herself stepping into the locker room and letting the door fall gently shut behind her. She glanced around. The smell of body odor tickled her nostrils but the scent of freshly-used showers helped curb it to a minimum. Or maybe that was just another new pregnancy symptom - a heightened sense of smell.

There was a large Gulls logo in the center of the carpet. It was bad luck to walk over the logo no matter who you were so she made sure to stay at the edge, taking in the beige wood. Each player had his space. A name plate was placed above each space and jerseys were hanging, ready to be plucked by the laundry crew to wash them at some point tonight.

Kyle was currently sitting at his place on the bench, a towel wrapped around his lower torso, his blond hair dark gold and dripping with drops, revealing a recent shower. He was bare chested, bare foot, sitting there seemingly deep in thought.

Emma wasn't sure if he knew she was there or not so she cleared her throat and remained standing where she was; across from him. He seemed like he might want space and she didn't want to push it if she didn't have to. Maybe she shouldn't have come in here at all.

He looked beautiful, if tragic, and her fingers itched to push back the damp hair from his face. Not that it was in his eyes, considering how short he liked to wear his hair, but they longed to run through his tresses, to touch him again.

He picked up his sky-blue eyes and when he saw her, they softened.

"Hey," he murmured, his voice crisp and desolate.

"Hey," she replied back. "You okay?" She quirked an eyebrow, leaning forward so her elbows rested on her knees. She gave him a soft, encouraging smile.

"You saw that game," he said, his tone bitter as he leaned back and all but snorted. He crossed his arms over his chest and Emma couldn't help but feel her eyes get drawn to his biceps that stretched when he did so. "I was shit."

"You were not -"

"Don't try to patronize me, Em," he snapped his eyes flashing into hers. "Please. Be honest with me."

Emma pressed her lips together. He wanted honesty. That was almost ironic, considering she had a big secret she probably should tell him but hadn't yet. Maybe she wouldn't anytime soon. She didn't know, wasn't sure. She hated this stupid game.

"Okay," she said slowly, her eyes dropping to the tips of her chucks. "You want honesty? You're letting them get into your head."

He blinked in surprise at her words but made no move to get defensive. In fact, if she was being honest, he almost seemed more receptive to what she had to say.

As such, she cleared her throat and forced herself to continue.

"You're letting them get into your head," she repeated. "You're thinking too much about playing and it looks like you aren't having fun anymore." She stopped, sucking out a breath and letting her hazel eyes rest on him. "Are you having fun?"

Kyle continued to look at her. If anyone else was in the room, they would have originally assumed he was staring at her blankly save for the intense burning in his sky-blue eyes. They might be concerned for her, perhaps he was angry with her for speaking honestly to him. However, she knew Kyle well enough to know that he wasn't angry. If anything, he was hearing her, he was listening what she was saying and taking her words in, digesting them, seeing how well they fit in his system. Finally, he pressed his lips together and looked away. Though he hadn't actually responded to her question, she knew his answer.

"Why not?" Emma asked in a soft voice. "I've seen you play, Kyle. Every single home game, I've been there. And even on an off-game, I've seen you have fun. I've watched you enjoy yourself. I've seen effort. But the past few weeks, ever since Vegas, it looks like you're at a job that you don't really like." She paused softly. "Why?"

"I don't know." His voice was right. He still looked away.

Emma felt compelled to move from her seat to sit next to him. She continued to keep her distance, she continued to refrain from touching him because she didn't want to smother him when she could tell he needed to be alone, at least for right now. Once he relaxed, she would feel it was more appropriate to touch him. Right now, this was about him, not about them as a couple.

"I think you're putting a lot of pressure on yourself," she

continued. "And you're analyzing it too much and thinking about it too much and then you mess up or make a bad decision."

Kyle pressed his lips together and nodded his head, his eyes on his bare feet. He clenched his jaw, causing it to pop.

"You need to stay out of the box," she told him.

"I know," he snapped then winced. Emma didn't flinch, didn't take it personally. She knew this wasn't about her, it was about him. She couldn't take his reaction personally. "I know," he repeated, more gently. "It's like, I'm caught flat-footed and I can't catch up so I reach out my stick. Or we're in the defensive zone and I'm trying to clear the puck, it goes over the glass directly."

"How do you think you can fix those mistakes?" Emma asked, sliding closer to him, still not touching him. He turned his head, his mouth still closed, but a question in his eyes. "When I see one of my students struggling, I have them take the next day off to do anything but dance. Distract themselves. Hopefully, it will rid them of the pressure they're feeling to get the steps right. When they come back, I explain that they are in control of their body. Not anyone or anything else. Which means they can take the necessary steps in order to correct their mistakes. Sometimes, that means practicing only the footwork. Sometimes, that means running and building stamina. Sometimes, that means visualizing the choreography. At the very least, they'll focus on something new, something different. A new way of looking at things really helps things fall into place." She stopped talking, allowing her words to sink in. "So what about you? What do you think you need to work on to improve?"

He was silent for a long minute and Emma thought he wasn't going to tell her anything. Kyle had always been reserved, even with her. There were rare occasions when he would open up to her and tell her how he was feeling, which was how she knew she was special, how she was different, compared to the other people in his life. For the most part, however, he kept his feelings to himself and Emma had always been okay with that. She had accepted that that was who he was and it had nothing to do with her and everything to do with him. Emma was the same way so it helped that neither expected the other to open up and share feelings.

However, maybe it was because of the new hormones racing through her body or maybe it was because of the fact that she hadn't really noticed things until now but she realized she wanted to speak to him about her feelings and she wanted him to open up more as well. She didn't want to be the couple that didn't say anything or share anything with each other; she wanted to feel comfortable telling him anything and she wanted him to do the same.

Emma also realized that just because that was what she wanted didn't necessarily mean that that was going to happen. She glanced down at her folded hands resting in her lap, before looking back at Kyle with hopeful eyes. She didn't realize how important it was that he answer her question; however, she also knew that this wasn't going to change overnight. And if she did want it to change, she needed to be the one to make the first move and show him what it meant to share feelings.

"You don't have to say anything," she told him, shrugging her shoulders. She felt uncomfortable with the silence, which was strange considering one of the things she was most attracted to Kyle was the fact that she was comfortable around him from the first time they officially met. And now, in this moment of intense silence where she was trying to help him and dig deeper into his playing issues, she was afraid he wasn't going to say anything. She was afraid he wasn't going to open up to her and share what was in his head, what was going on with him, what he was thinking about, what he was worrying about. And that scared her because she realized she wanted to know these things. She wanted to be the one he confided in, regardless of whether or not he preferred to keep his mouth closed and his feelings to himself.

She wanted to be his exception.

"No," Kyle said, shaking his head before picking it up so he could lock eyes with her. "It's not that. I'm just thinking about what you said."

Emma nodded, pressing her lips together to keep from saying anything that might cause her to stick her foot in her mouth. She needed to be patient with him and if he chose not to share anything, she would have to accept it and maybe talk to him about at another time.

"I've been slacking off when it comes to skating," he finally said, reaching behind him to cup the back of his neck with his hand. "I could do a lot more with my skating. I could push myself. I could run more and keep active. I could go to more optional skates." He looked back at her, a small quirk to his lips as he regarded her. "I guess I've been slacking off a bit. It's hard to stay focused when I've been distracted."

Emma felt her cheeks turn pink and she laughed despite herself. "Are you saying I'm the reason for your play the past few weeks? I don't think so, buddy."

He laughed and pulled Emma to him so she was straddling his lap and locked her wrists around his neck. "It's the truth," he said, his voice dropping and his sky-blue eyes turning dark as he looked into hers. His hands gripped her hips and held her possessively.

Emma sighed in his grasp, feeling both desire and safe at the same time. She could feel his hardness press against her through the thick towel he was wearing and she bit her bottom lip, feeling her eyes darken with her own lust and her heart race against her chest.

There was no way he intended to take her in the locker room, where anybody could walk in - including the janitors, who were due in a few minutes.

But then he started kissing her neck, in the most sensitive

spot behind her ear and her eyes rolled back and nearly all rational thought left her mind, at least temporarily.

"What about," she managed to get out, breathless. "What about Taboo?"

"I don't care about Taboo when I have the most beautiful woman on my lap and only a towel between us," he growled and she gasped.

It wasn't long before he had her panting. Her clothes were shed and his hands were all over her skin, cupping her hips, running up and down her back, getting lost in her hair. She felt her thighs moisten at his gentle caresses, could feel her pelvis thrum with anticipation feeling his hardness press against her.

God, she loved making love to Kyle Underwood. She never doubted he had the experience to please any woman but there was something about him that made her burn with desire, lose her breath, want him more than she could ever know.

It was only when he had positioned himself inside of her, angling his cock so it hit her in just the right spot that she dug her nails into his back and shuddered out a breath, when she realized they were having sex without a condom on.

She should tell him, she knew. It didn't matter that she was already pregnant and therefore couldn't get pregnant, but Kyle didn't know that. However, considering how deeply he had buried himself inside of her, she didn't think the thought had even crossed his mind. Maybe she didn't have to remind him since there were really no other consequences she could think of. Kyle got tested every year and once they decided to have sex, they both got tested beforehand and shared the results with each other. She also knew he was faithful. The only consequence that could come from unprotected sex was pregnancy.

And that had already happened.

So she let herself relax and enjoy this time with Kyle. She allowed herself to really feel what it was like to make love without any restrictions or barriers. The connection she felt with Kyle in the moment was indescribable. She hated to admit it, but there really was a difference between protection and not having protection. And when they came, she shattered and clutched him to her, taking as much of him as she could get. They didn't stop until they were both spent. And then they rushed to get dressed so they wouldn't get caught.

Chapter 5

THE NEXT MORNING, Emma waited until her father had already left for work before calling her general physician and asking to make an appointment to confirm her pregnancy.

"You know," the medical technician said, "we're just going to give you a pregnancy test and tell you the result. If you took one at home, there's really no need to get it confirmed. What we can do is refer you to some OBGYN's who specialize in pregnancy, labor and delivery and who are also in network and you can make an appointment with them as soon as possible."

Emma agreed and wrote down the three names and phone numbers the technician gave her.

After doing her research, she called up the first one - a Dr. Candace Howe located just across the street from Hoag Hospital, the nearest hospital to her home and, most likely, where she was going to deliver - if she was keeping the baby.

A voice in her head snorted. 'You know you're keeping the baby,' it muttered. 'Stop kidding yourself.'

The phone call to Dr. Howe's office lasted roughly fifteen minutes. They obviously took her insurance information and basic information including a name, a birth date, her smoking and drinking history, any allergies. They asked about her menstrual history, the day of her last period, and gave her the due date of November 9 - which could potentially change after her first ultrasound based on the size of the fetus.

Surprisingly enough, they scheduled her roughly two weeks from now, which was odd considering Emma thought this was something doctors would try to fit her in same day - or at the very least, same week.

"Yes, but we can't pick up baby's heart beat until roughly six weeks," the technician pointed out. "On the off chance that your dates are wrong - perhaps you ovulated later than an average cycle would indicate - we want to ensure that you come in and hear your baby's heart and be able to see baby on the ultrasound. This is why we push back the first appointments to roughly seven to eight weeks in pregnancy because if the dates are off, you're still likely to hear the heartbeat."

This made sense to Emma now that everything was explained.

The technician referred her to 'What to Expect' if there were things she wanted to know about or was curious as to what to expect. She also told Emma not to read stories online because each pregnancy was subjective.

Finally, she gave Emma a list of food she couldn't eat, activities she couldn't partake in, and when to call the doctor or go to the emergency room.

By the time Emma got off the phone, her head was swimming with overwhelm. She shook it, trying to get a hold of her swirling thoughts. She never thought pregnancy was easy, but now that she was experiencing this for herself, she realized just how complicated it could be.

At that moment, her phone pinged with an email. She glanced down and noticed it was from her doctor's office.

Congratulations on your pregnancy!

Emma had to press her lips together to keep from reacting. Why did people naturally assume all pregnancies were wanted?

Did that make her a bitch for even thinking? She clenched her jaw and looked away. She hoped not. It was hard for her to even admit she might want to keep this child - she kept going back and forth, back and forth. Her talk with Harper hadn't much helped, and it wasn't Harper's fault, it was because Emma was looking for someone to tell her what to do. She needed guidance, direction, because for the first time in nearly her whole life, she wasn't in control and she didn't know the right course of action.

The only other time she felt that way was when her mother left. She had only been three at the time so she barely remembered the woman who gave birth to her, but she did remember the loss she had felt, that hole in her heart that was still there, even today.

A year ago, one of her cousins on her mother's side had visited because she had wanted to meet Emma after all this time, but Emma refused. Her life was perfect, as far as she was concerned, and introducing a figure who had voluntarily left was not something she wanted to do. She didn't know how it would affect her life and, quite frankly, she didn't particularly care. As mean and as rude and as heartless as it sounded, she did not care about her mother. About the woman who chose to abandon her and her father. This person didn't get to choose when she was part of her daughter's life. Just because they were biologically related did not mean anything, at least not to Emma.

Her eyes skimmed the email. It was basically consisted of everything they had just discussed over the phone, including the foods she wasn't allowed to eat, information about spotting, bleeding, and cramping during the first trimester, and what to expect from her first prenatal appointment.

Four days before your appointment, you will be notified of a medical survey you must complete before your appointment. It will ask you for your medical history, your partner's medical history, and your family medical history on both sides. Please be as detailed as possible.

Emma's eyes widened. Both sides of her family? She clenched her jaw and clocked off her phone. She did not want to talk to her mom about anything, especially not about being pregnant. Maybe she didn't need to. What about all the adopted mom's having their own children who didn't know anything about their parents.

She clenched her jaw. There was no way she was going to get in contact with her mother if she didn't have to. Even if she had a way - Justin and her uncle had left a contact number with her father on the slim chance that Emma wanted to reach out to her mother - that didn't mean she would. In fact, once her cousin had left, Emma had instructed her father to trash the note. Trash the number. Trash everything that had to do with her mother. She didn't think he did. Her father knew when she was going based off of emotion and when she was being serious but it felt good saying it and pretending her father had actually listened to her.

"Hey."

She jumped, seeing her father in the doorway. He furrowed his brow upon seeing her jumpy reaction and tilted his head to the side.

"You okay?" he asked, his voice slightly hesitant. "You seem tense."

She shook her head, trying to calm her erratic heartbeat. "I just have a lot on my mind," she told him. "You're here early."

"Yeah," he agreed, nodding and closing the door behind him. "I finished a briefing and instead of heading back to the office, I decided to head home." He placed his briefcase on the dining table before heading to the living room and sinking into the leather theatre chairs her father had insisted they buy despite how expensive they were. "How are you feeling?"

"Honestly, Dad?" she said, feeling her resolve slip. Even if she couldn't tell her dad everything about what was going on with her, she could at least tell him what was going on in her head. "I'm stressed out. I have this thing growing inside of me and I don't know how to handle it."

"Choreography has always lived inside of you since you could walk," her father pointed out from his chair. Emma was holding her breath thanks to her poor choice in words but it seemed to go over her father's head. Thank God. "The best thing you can do is bring it out. Sometimes it's scared to breathe life into your creation because you're not sure if it's going to be as perfect as you imagined it or because you're worried how people will perceive you once it's out there, but you have to have faith in your audience and you have to have faith in yourself. You can do wonderful, extraordinary things, Em. I don't think you realize how incredible you are."

Emma felt her eyes tear up and she immediately blinked them away. Damn these stupid hormones. They were going to give her away.

"How was work?" she forced herself to ask, doing her best to ensure her voice didn't come out shaky.

"Work," he said. "You know how it is. I go to trial next week. I just hope it doesn't run late, what with the Gulls finally making the playoffs." He shrugged and flipped on CNN. "We'll see, though." He glanced over his shoulder. "Shouldn't you be at rehearsal right now?"

"Shit!" she exclaimed, glancing at her watch. He was right. She was supposed to be at her studio a half an hour ago. She ran up the stairs and to her room and quickly threw on yoga pants and a tank top, tossed her hair into a messy ponytail, and slipped into an old pair of Nikes. Then, she bounded down the stairs, called a goodbye over to her father - who was laughing incessantly - and headed to her car. It was a beat up Mercedes-Benz that she loved more than the majority of her possessions.

Her studio - Once Upon A Dance - was located on the border of Newport Beach and Costa Mesa, in a nice neighbor-hood with a small shopping center where parents could pick up groceries while their children did an hour of dance.

The studio was something that didn't turn over a profit just yet - Emma had it open from five to eight Monday through Friday's unless there was a Gulls' game. Then, she modified the hours so she could attend the home games while still getting her students in appropriately. It was a small suite with mirrors and hardwood floor. When her father first leased the building for Emma, Emma put a lot of her money into fixing the place up and creating the studio she had always dreamed of dancing in. She usually trained one age group for one hour two to three times a week. Everyone from toddlers to teenagers had classes offered at her studio and her classes filled up quickly. She was surprised she broke even the majority of the months in terms of cost - there were even a few months she had generated a profit.

Since she was the only instructor on staff, she paid herself a small salary but she didn't have to worry about hiring anyone else - at least, not yet. She had been hoping to sell the studio when she left for New York but now that she wouldn't be dancing on Broadway like she planned for her whole life, she wasn't sure what she intended to do with the studio now.

She managed to get there just before her first hour - toddlers - began and dove into three hours of light dance and more training. It helped get her mind off of her current worries and she found herself smiling and laughing and enjoying being in the moment.

Once the last student left, she proceeded to start shutting down the studio. At that moment, she was struck with an over-whelming urge to vomit - an urge she didn't resist. She ran to the restroom and heaved up the small dinner she had had between sessions. Once she finished and flushed the toilet, she leaned back against the door and took a moment to catch her breath.

So the symptoms begin...

Chapter 6

THE NEXT DAY, Emma went to Barnes & Noble and decided to browse the pregnancy books. Her eyes lingered on 'What to Expect' and she picked it up, deciding to flip through this so-called pregnancy bible. It was thick, with relatively small font. From what she could tell, each chapter was broken up by each month of pregnancy. There were expectations by week and common questions at the end that might crop up which would potentially affect her.

She pushed her brows up, continuing to flip through it. It seemed filled with information, information she desperately wanted. However, having this book would definitely be a big obvious indication that she was pregnant.

"Emma?"

Emma jumped and whirled around. She found herself looking into a pair of crystal blue eyes.

Zachary Ryan.

"Hey," she said, snapping the book shut and trying to hide it behind her back. His eyes followed her gesture and he tilted his head to the side. "What, what are you doing here?"

He cocked his lips into the arrogant smirk he was known for

and tilted his head to the side. The man was like a Greek god, his face chiseled, his blue eyes sharp and crisp. He was tall as well, towering over Emma's five foot three frame and was built with solid muscle. It was no wonder why women fell at his feet but regardless, he seemed completely smitten with Harper.

"Despite my profession, I do like to read," he told her, his tone only slightly sarcastic.

Emma's lips quirked up. "Of course," she replied, and then cleared her throat.

"You okay?" he asked her. "Harper told me... don't be mad at her, we tell each other everything. Plus, in her defense, I did find you in this section of the bookstore..." He pushed his brows up and crossed his arms over his chest.

"You're not going to tell Kyle, are you?" Emma asked, her eyes wide with worry. She knew Zach and Kyle and Alec were best friends. They had their guys night every other week where they got together at someone's place, shot pool, and smoked cigars. She wasn't sure where guys drew the line in regards to what was private and what they kept to themselves. Being pregnant was a big deal and she knew Zach probably wanted to tell his friend because Kyle deserved to know but that didn't necessarily mean he would.

"Are you kidding?" Zach asked, pushing his brows together. "Harper would murder me." He shook his head. "No, I'm not going to say anything. And she specifically told me not to tell you what to do, but if I could at least give some advice?"

Emma hid a smirk, nodding her head.

"Kyle has a lot going on," Zach pointed out. He pressed his lips together, trying to think of the right words to say. Emma appreciated the thought he was putting into this. "I'm sure you've noticed that his game is off, for whatever reason. And it has been for a while. Between you and me, Cherney's thinking about dropping him to the third line next game since the second line is doing so well." He placed his hands on his hips, his shoulders pushed up. "I don't know what's going on between the two of you except this, obviously, but since Kyle doesn't know about it, I highly doubt his play is a result of that."

Emma nodded, not quite sure how else to respond to that statement. It was true; Kyle had no idea about the pregnancy, and unless he remembered that they had had unprotected sex and was concerned about the consequences of that, there was nothing between them that had changed. They were the same.

"You don't think," Emma said slowly. She cut herself off and shook her head, looking away. But then, she forced herself to finish the thought. "You don't think he did something."

Zach took a step back and Emma could tell his guard went up. She winced.

"Forget I asked," she told him. "Just forget it. I know there's this whole bros before hos mentality that is especially prevalent in the hockey world."

Zach shook his head. "It has nothing to do with that, actually," he said. "If anyone said anything about Harper, I would beat the shit out of them, no problem. No hesitation. I've only known Kyle half a year. You know him even better than I do. Do you think Kyle is that type of person?"

Emma felt her cheeks turn pink. She shook her head. "I don't think he'd be unfaithful," she told him. "And if he had, I wouldn't put you in an awkward position and make you feel compelled to share it with me." She pressed her lips together. "We have talked about his play, though. He definitely isn't in denial about the past few weeks."

"No one is harder on Kyle than Kyle himself," he agreed. "And I know that he needs support more than anything."

Emma nodded. "He also needs honesty," she murmured more to herself than to him. "I tried to bullshit him once and he bit my head off."

Zach chuckled. "Yeah, I can see that happening," he agreed.

Emma paused, giving Zach a quizzical look. "Do you mind if I ask you a question?" she asked, tilting her head to the side.

"Shoot."

"Harper said you and her have actually talked about marriage and kids even though you've only been dating five or six months," Emma pointed out.

"Yeah," Zach said slowly.

Emma wasn't quite sure how to finish that up. She believed the question spoke for itself. However, when he continued to stare at her with a blank expression on in face, she refrained from rolling her eyes and said, "Why?"

He seemed confused by the question due to the way he furrowed his brow and cocked his head to the side. "Why not?" he asked.

She let out a huff of a breath. "How do you even know she's the one?" Emma asked. "Listen, Harper is one of my best friends. I'm crazy about her. She's amazing and you're lucky to have her. But how did you know she was the one to start talking about marriage and babies and all that stuff that makes a relationship serious?"

Zach pressed his lips together, teasing the tip of his chin with his fingers, deep in thought. "Honestly?" he asked, locking eyes with her once again. "I can't explain it. It's just a feeling you get when you've met the right one. Look, I know that sounds cheesy and scripted but it's the truth. Harper's the kind of girl you meet once in a blue moon, probably even less. She's the kind of girl who can be one of the guys but also dress up and be beautiful and feminine and everything I could possibly desire. She's my dream girl, really. And I'm lucky enough to realize this and know that she is the person I want to spend the rest of my life with. At the very least we can talk about our future together and what that means to each other and how we affect each other and how we support each other. I don't want to lose her and I know she doesn't want to lose me. Relationships aren't going to be perfect. Harper is not perfect. But somehow, she is perfect for me. All of those little things that previous guys might have found annoying, I find endearing. And yeah, maybe it's because this relationship is still so new and it's in the honeymoon phase. I can understand that. But regardless of all of that, I know without a doubt. That she's the one. I don't care who I am. I'm never going to find anyone better than her." He wrinkled his brow. "Does that help you at all?"

Emma hesitated before nodding once. "Does Harper feel the same way about you?" she asked, her voice tentative. This wasn't any of her business but she felt good talking to Zach and getting a male perspective on everything.

"I'm confident that she does," he told her, "but that's not the point of being in love. You don't care how the other one feels because their feelings don't dictate yours.

You love because you don't have a choice, because you can't do anything but love. It's not waiting around for Kyle to love you first. Does that make sense?"

Emma nodded her head.

"Let me ask you a question, Em," he said, "and obviously this will be between you and me. I get the feeling that both you and Kyle are at a comfortable point in your relationship where you're serious, you're monogamous, and you genuinely care about each other but you have yet to make serious plans for the future. I know you're going to Regina over the off-season to meet his parents - which is great -but don't you think it's odd it's taken nearly two years before you go back to his home town to meet his family?"

"He hasn't really met my dad, either, as my boyfriend, I mean," Emma said slowly before taking her bottom lip and teasing it between her teeth. "He hasn't really asked. And neither have I."

"That's my point!" Zach exclaimed, causing some of the onlookers to glance at him. He didn't seem to notice. He also seemed to have forgotten he was in a bookstore. "You're not supposed to ask, Em. Come on. You care about someone, you do something for them. You shouldn't be worried how they're going to interpret it. If you do, then you're with the wrong person. Or you're overthinking things. You need to relax and enjoy your relationship. Don't be afraid to be romantic. Kyle isn't big on public displays of affection but he's an extremely loyal person and if you do some kind of grand gesture that shows this, shows how much you care and how loyal you are to him, he'll feel more comfortable letting his guard down. And once he does that, he's yours."

"Are you saying he's not mine now?" Emma asked, tilting her head to the side.

Zach shook his head. "It's not that," he told her. "You guys are at a safe place in your relationship. Do you want it to go deeper? Or are you okay with mediocrity?"

"Are you saying my relationship is mediocre?" Emma asked, not bothering to hide the defensiveness from her tone.

Zach glanced away. "I feel as though I'm saying the wrong things," he said slowly. "Listen, you asked me how I knew Harper was the one, right? I guess it's because I don't ever want to be safe with her. I feel safe with her but I don't ever want us to be safe when we could take a risk and be so much more. You have to decide if Kyle is worth the risk." He pushed up his brows. "Do you understand what I'm saying?"

Emma locked eyes with Zach and nodded. "I think I do," she told him honestly. "Well, I'll let you get back to shopping. I really appreciate you taking the time to talk to me about this stuff." She cocked her lips into a small smile. "Thanks. And I'm happy for you and Harper."

"No problem," he said, placing a hand on her shoulder. "And let me give you some advice: trust Kyle because he is worth the risk. And if you don't think so or you're not sure, then you don't deserve him."

Chapter 7

EMMA FOUND HERSELF THAT NIGHT, looking at herself in the full-length mirror. She was in a simple summer dress, red in color. The sleeves were t-shirt, the length about an inch above her knee. It was tight and dipped low in front, revealing nice cleavage thanks to a push-up bra. Her breasts tingled, however, but Emma was aware that this was a common symptom during pregnancy and she was actually looking forward to her boobs getting bigger.

She was just past six weeks along, with her doctor's appointment next week. If all went well, she would hear her baby's heart beat for the first time. Her heart skipped a beat just thinking about it.

Truth be told, Emma was surprised how quickly she had accepted having this child. Now, instead of dreading things, she was looking forward to them. Doctor's appointments, seeing her baby on an ultrasound for the first time.

She gnawed her bottom lip, realizing that she got to experience this excitement but Kyle did not. Because she hadn't told him yet. And she wasn't sure if and when she planned to tell him. She knew she would eventually, she just didn't know when. And how.

Tonight, they were going to a romantic dinner on the beach. There was a small beachside bistro on one side of PCH that overlooked the water. Kyle had an in because Dimitri Petrov was primary owner of the restaurant and always got his team tables should they request it. The bistro had food and drinks named after him and his family but now that he was going through a divorce, Emma wondered if he was going to keep the Terra, a chocolate alcoholic drink named after his now ex-wife.

Not that it was any of Emma's business. She had met Dimitri Petrov a handful of times before and after her relationship with Kyle. Her father attended every single charity event the Gulls hosted including a golfing tournament, a beach day, an auction, and a fashion show - which was scheduled a couple of weeks from now. He always dragged her along because he really didn't have anyone else to take and because he felt that they could bond over this experience together.

Dimitri Petrov was the nicest guy on the ice. He was deliriously handsome for his age - aging gracefully like wine - and had an adorable accent that as hard to decipher at times. Even now, Emma had no idea how the hell anyone could leave Dimitri, especially since it was known that cheating - at least on his part - wasn't what broke them up.

Kyle had invited her out tonight because he seemed to think they hadn't been spending a lot of time together since their Vegas trip due to the fact that they were both so busy with their individual careers. It was his way of reconnecting and deepening their bond.

She could appreciate that but that didn't mean she wasn't concerned about what was going on with him. She knew he wasn't the type of person to cheat. Yes, he enjoyed the single life before her but every girl he was with knew that going into the fling they had. Once he and Emma got together, after months of being friends, he immediately dropped his previous lifestyle cold-turkey. Even though girls clamored for his attention, he never strayed. He never even seemed tempted.

Now, though...

Was his poor play a result of guilt? Even if he hadn't cheated, had he done something else that made him feel guilty? That affected his play this much?

She wanted to ask him but didn't think she should. If he was going to tell her, he would. No question. Right?

It wasn't as though she was going out of her way to tell him about being pregnant, even though he had a right to know. Even though she should.

And that caused a block in her dancing. She couldn't finish the damn piece she had been working on for the past two weeks. She thought it was because of her pregnancy, because she had a lot going on and wasn't quite sure how to handle everything. Now, though... maybe it wasn't as clear-cut as she thought. Maybe she needed to be around Kyle. Maybe they needed to trust each other more with what was going on in their lives.

"Thanks for coming out," Kyle said after the hostess left them with menus and a promise that the waiter would be there soon. "I know how busy you are with your recital coming up."

"Actually," Emma remarked, opening the menu, her eyes immediately going over to the specials. "I can't finish this piece to save my life. I'm completely blocked. My students are hounding me for an ending and I can't seem to give one to them."

"What kind of ending do they want?" Kyle asked. He leaned casually back against his chair, not even cracking open the menu. He had been here enough times to know what he wanted.

"It's not about what they want," Emma replied. She hoped she didn't sound defensive. It wasn't her intention to do so. "It's about what's right for the piece. It needs to fit."

Kyle's lips quirked up but he made no comment on her

words. It was almost as though he was amused by her phrasing, as though she wasn't talking about the piece.

"Anyway," she said hurriedly, setting down the menu. "I have a lot of work I need to do, considering the recital is four weeks away and these kids need time to perfect it."

"They aren't going to perfect it, Em," Kyle pointed out gently.

"Nothing will ever be perfect."

Emma pressed her lips together, feeling her heart jump in her throat. "Yeah," she said with a slow nod. "You're right about that."

"But that's okay," Kyle said. "That's what makes life fun - the unexpected. Life's little imperfections make things unique. So one kid isn't pointing their toes and hitting their mark or whatever else dance deals with."

Emma giggled as the waiter came back with a wine sample for both of them. Immediately, the smile slid off of her face and her eyes went wide. She had no idea what to do. She couldn't drink. She wasn't even going to fake it, unwilling to take that risk and potentially harm the baby. But she needed to get out of this without making it obvious as to why.

"N-no thank you," she stuttered, moving the wine glass before the waiter could pour her a sample. She nearly knocked the glass down. "Sorry, I, uh, I'm on a strict diet to keep me focused until this whole recital thing is over." She was speaking more to Kyle than to the waiter, her words coming out jumbled and shaky just like her hands.

"It's just a sample," Kyle said, narrowing his sky-blue eyes and cocking his head to the side.

"You okay?"

"I'm getting sick of everyone asking me that, to be honest," she muttered, more to herself than to him.

"We're concerned about you, Emma," Kyle pointed out, his tone slightly defensive. "What do you expect? Are we not allowed to ask if you're okay? You aren't acting like yourself and I don't think it has to do with your spring recital."

"Oh, just because it's not hockey doesn't make it any less important to me," Emma said, trying to keep her voice down so they wouldn't attract onlookers. "Dancing is my life. Well, it was before I started dating you. Then, everything started revolving around your schedule. Our dates, my recitals, my practices. I was looking forward to New York because then it would be about me. Me and me alone. But it's not. Not anymore."

Kyle narrowed his eyes. "What do you mean, go to New York?" he asked.

Emma felt her throat dry up. She hadn't told him, she remembered. She wasn't planning on telling him until she got her acceptance letter. If she got an acceptance letter.

"For dance," she told him, forcing herself to look into his eyes. He deserved that much. "My dream has always been to dance on Broadway."

He seemed surprised. His eyes went to his lap as though he was searching for something there, something Emma wasn't quite sure what he was looking for.

"Why," he began, picking his eyes up. They were filled with an emotion Emma had never seen in them before - hurt. And she was the cause of it. "Why wouldn't you tell me?"

Emma shrugged, feeling herself get increasingly more and more uncomfortable. "I just," she said. "I didn't want to bring it up unless I was accepted. You already have so much on your plate, I didn't want to add to it."

"That is such bullshit, Emma," he said through a harsh whisper. He was already socially awkward on a good day. Now that things were tense between them in a public place, he was doing his best to keep control over his emotions in order to calm himself down, to not make a scene, to not get more and more people to look at them.

Her eyes widened at his accusation. "Excuse me?" she asked, trying to keep her voice down, more out of respect for Kyle rather than because she cared whether or not people looked at them during their tiff. She had never been one of those girls who cared one way or the other if she made a scene - though she did try to avoid it as much as she could - but she knew how uncomfortable Kyle was in the public eye so she always made sure she kept her behavior in check so they wouldn't be noticed as much.

"You heard me," he said, his teeth clenched together so his voice came out tight. "It's bullshit. You should have told me you were doing something like applying to dance academies in New York because your dream is to dance on Broadway. Don't you think that as your boyfriend, that's something you should have told me? Don't I deserve that much?"

Emma opened her mouth to reply. She knew what she wanted to say but knew it wouldn't help matters. "You never asked," she said anyway.

He gave her a look, like he couldn't quite believe she had said that, and then glanced away in disgust. "I shouldn't have to," he told her as though it was the most obvious thing in the world. "I'm your boyfriend. Or, at least, I thought I was." Without warning, he threw his keys on the table and abruptly stood. "I've got to get some air. You can drive yourself home."

"Kyle, I-" Emma began but Kyle was already making his way out of the restaurant.

Chapter 8

WHEN EMMA PARKED Kyle's car in front of her house, she unbuckled her seatbelt, placed her arms over the steering wheel, and started to cry. She didn't know if it was the pregnancy hormones or the fact that she felt like a complete idiot. She saw the hurt that flashed across Kyle's eyes when she told him about New York - something she hadn't actually meant to do. Not until she knew for sure.

But now, she realized what a fool she had been. Emma had purposefully kept that secret from Kyle because she didn't want to share her dreams with anyone. No one knew about New York except for her father. Why wouldn't she tell her boyfriend of nearly two years? Unless she didn't wholly trust Kyle. But that didn't make sense because there was no reason for her not to trust him. He was trustworthy and dutiful and always there when she needed him. And she... well, she assumed that eventually, he would leave, just like her mother did. Which was why she kept him at an arm's length. She didn't invite him to recitals, thinking it would be a bother since it sometimes clashed with his hockey schedule. She didn't invite him to eat dinner with her and her father for the same reason. They did date every now and then - go out by themselves dressed up and romantic. They didn't spend holidays together - a lot of the time, he was traveling anyway.

Why didn't this bother her until now?

Probably because she was okay with this safe relationship, superficial in all its commitment. When push came to shove, though, they weren't really boyfriend or girlfriend, were they? Not when they didn't share things with each other. Not when they didn't trust each other enough to open up.

And sure, Kyle did have hockey to focus on, but he always made it clear just how much he loved her and how lucky he was to be with her. To the point where he was allowing her to dictate this relationship and where it went. He wanted to be with her in whatever way she would take him. And she chose to keep him out.

Because she was afraid.

She wasn't certain how long she cried for but she did know her nose was blotchy, her face was wet with tears and mucus, and her head hurt more than it had in a long time. When she finally ran out of tears to cry, she continued to hiccup, her entire body expelling the hiccup with jumping shoulders and a stuffed nose.

By the time Emma walked into the house, it was well past eleven o'clock. She expected her father to be in his office, looking at paperwork for his latest case or sleeping. Instead, he was on the couch, reading a newspaper - one of the last people to do so - almost as though he was waiting for her. When he heard the click of the door, he lowered the newspaper and gave Emma a small smile.

"I've been waiting for you to come in," he told her, his lips quirking up into a small smile.

She sniffles. Any hope of hiding her tears or the fact that she had been crying for a good duration of time went out the window. She felt his eyes on her face, noting the dropping mascara, the red face, the tear-stained cheeks, the crusted nose. She was a disaster.

"How did you know I'd even be back this soon?" she asked through a hiccup.

"To be honest," her father murmured, folding the paper, setting it down on the coffee table, and removing his thin-rimmed reading glasses, "Kyle called me and told me that the two of you got into a bit of a tiff at the restaurant. He wanted me to text him when you got home just to make sure that you made it home safely."

Before she could stop herself, her eyes started to fill tears. She immediately looked away, hoping her father wouldn't notice. The problem with her father was that, as a lawyer, he noticed everything.

"Em?" he asked, slowly standing up and keeping his sharp eyes on her. "You okay? I know Kyle said you guys had a tiff. Do you want to talk about it?"

Emma shook her head, trying to maintain control of herself. Her face was sore, her eyes were exhausted, and her headache was starting to come back. She hated crying so damn much and yet she couldn't control these emotions no matter how hard she tried.

"Well, can I hug you until you stop crying?" he asked, slowly coming over to her, reaching his arms out. Emma didn't hesitate to step into the hug her father offered and buried her face in his plain white t-shirt. It would probably be ruined after her cry but he didn't seem to mind. "When you're ready to talk - if you're ready to talk - I'm here for you, okay?"

She nodded in his chest and let the emotion pour out of her, not bothering to try and push it away anymore. Not when she felt so safe.

It took a few moments - not nearly as long as the first time - but Emma finally felt herself start to wind down. Her father gently led her over to the couch so they could sit together and relax as best as they could.

"I've never been the one to claim I have a sense of intuition," he began slowly, his voice a gentle murmur against her ear, "but it seems to me that something is troubling you." He pulled his head away from hers, his eyes going over her face. She knew he was looking for any tell he could find, any indication of what she had in her mind. "I'm not an expert in everything. I hardly say the right things at the right time and even when I try, it all comes out wrong. But I'm still your dad. I'm still here for you when you need me, even if that's not right now."

Emma's heart broke and she felt herself cry even harder than she had been before. She felt her father tense and she knew he was taking it personally, as though he was the one who was causing the tears. And, in a way, he was. But not because he meant to. Not because of malice or ill-intentions. He was saying exactly what she needed to hear right now.

"Dad," she said, sniffling as best as she could. Her head was completely clogged and she wanted nothing more than to take off her clothes and crawl under her covers, feeling the cool, smooth sheets caress her skin. Instead, she forced herself to continue, forced herself to admit what she hadn't admitted to anyone save for Harper. "Dad, I really messed up and I don't know what to do about it."

There was a heartbeat of silence. He tensed as he continued to hold her, continued to offer her whatever comfort he could.

"Okay," he finally said slowly. She knew the worst case scenarios were going off in his head and she couldn't help but wonder if unplanned pregnancy was part of those scenarios. "What, exactly, did you do, Emma? You didn't cheat on Kyle, did you?"

"What?" Emma pushed off her father and gave him a watery glare. "No, Dad, I did not cheat on the man I love, thank you very much."

"Well, excuse me," her father replied. "You said worst case. I'm just going with what you've given me." He gave her a sideways look. "You didn't hit him or verbally abuse him, did you?"

Emma nearly laughed at that insinuation. "No, Dad," she told him. "You know I don't fight typically. At least, not with my hands."

"That's why I added verbal abuse," he pointed out.

"Clearly, you're kidding," she said.

He raised his brows, a dry look on his face. "Clearly."

He nudged her with his shoulder. "Tell me." Then, quieter, he added, "Please."

"Dad," she said, taking a deep breath. She picked her eyes up and locked onto his. She wanted him to see how serious she was. "I'm pregnant."

There was a tight breath, sucking in sharply, tight and tension-filled. She could feel her father shift beside her, his entire body tense. Just like the air. She could count the heart beats sounding off in her head.

She let out a shaky breath, needing him to say something. Anything.

"Okay," he finally managed to get out. He nodded his head once. "Okay. So what you're saying is you have a child in-" he stopped, closed his eyes, shook his head, gritted his teeth so his jaw popped. Opened his eyes, took a breath. "I don't want to think about how it happened. Would you mind telling me why it happened?"

Emma nodded. While his voice came out muffled and tight, at least he sounded... open. Open to the possibility that she didn't mean for this and she was coming to him for help. For guidance.

"A stupid mistake," she said, speaking quickly. "Do you really want to know the details? It happened in Vegas, I think. It's the only time we -" She cut herself off. Even though her father was an adult and she was an adult did not make it any easier to talk about sex with him. She might have trusted him with her life but that didn't mean she was able to talk about this sort of thing with him. "We were both tipsy."

"You don't drink," he said flatly.

"When you're in Vegas..." She let her voice trail off and shrugged her shoulders.

"Well, clearly it doesn't always stay in Vegas, does it?" he snapped and then winced. "I didn't mean to snap. Emma, you always have a good head on your shoulders. You're entitled to mess up every once in a while. But this isn't some mess up to be taken lightly. Does Kyle know?"

She shook her head, biting her bottom lip. "I haven't told him yet," she told him.

"Oh." A suck in of breath, like a small vacuum. "Do you plan on it?"

"Dad," Emma said, shaking her head. "I have no idea what my plan is, to be honest. I have no idea what I'm going to do. I just... I just need time to process this. I have nine months, right?"

"Honey, you're having a baby," her father pointed out. "You need to make choices now. You need to figure out what you're going to do. But I'm here for you, okay? I'm here."

He pulled her into a hug, and for the moment, that was all Emma needed.

Chapter 9

KYLE DIDN'T CALL her the next day. Not that Emma expected him to. She had been an asshole about the whole New York thing and instead of at least acknowledging his feelings, she got defensive. She pushed him away, even further away than she kept him since they first got together.

The problem was, she hadn't even realized she had been doing it until that blowout. She thought she was doing him a favor by purposefully not putting pressure on involving him in certain aspects of her life so he could focus on his hockey game. She realized, however, that ultimately, it kept him away from knowing who she really was. And not because he wanted but because he didn't have a choice. Not if she was making these decisions.

More than that, Emma was kept out of certain parts of his life as a result. How was she supposed to know how he'd react to her dancing or to her applying to New York or even about the issues she had with her mother if she never gave him the opportunity.

"What's the problem, Em?" her father finally asked her that evening over dinner. Emma had made spaghetti with ground beef, something she loved. She had already topped the pasta with a heap of Parmesan cheese - her favorite part. She needed comfort food right now. She needed to feel as good as she could.

"Honestly, Dad?" Emma asked, dropping her fork so it clattered against the plate and dropped her head into her hands. "I really messed things up with Kyle. This entire time that I've been with him, I never even told him I wanted to dance on Broadway." She picked her head up, furrowing her brow as she looked directly in front of her. "Like, why? Why wouldn't I tell him that? That's something even my friends know. Why would I keep that from him?"

Her father finished chewing his spaghetti and then wiped his mouth with the paper napkin. "Well," he said slowly. "What do you think it is?"

Emma shrugged, letting her head hang down. "I have no idea," she said through a groan before shaking her head. "I just, I didn't want to distract him from his game."

"Or," her father said slowly, "and, please, take this with a grain of salt because I'm an old man who hasn't experienced love in a very, very long time, but indulge me: maybe you're using his hockey as an excuse when, in reality, he has never given you any indication of that at all and you're seeing what you want to see."

"Why would I want to see that?" she asked, turning her head to lock eyes with him.

"Because you're afraid to get close to anyone," he pointed out, his voice gentle and not judgmental. "Because the one person who's supposed to be there for you always left without a word, without a reason. And you're afraid of letting anyone close to you."

"And you're the exception?" she asked, raising a skeptical brow.

"I'm not going to take your attitude personally," he told her in a breezy tone. "I've been the one person who's been in your life since you were born. You had no choice but to let me be close to you."

Emma chewed her bottom lip, dropping her eyes to her lap as she tried to get comfortable in her father's oversized theatre seats.

"I think it doesn't help matters that you have an added responsibility you have to consider," he pointed out gently, replacing his eyes onto her still-flat stomach. She felt her cheeks pinch; it felt weird knowing that he knew about her pregnancy. Before him, only Harper knew about the pregnancy but that was never much of an issue because she wasn't around enough to make it a reality.

Her father, on the other hand, was constantly in her life. For the most part, she saw him every morning and every evening. They always tried to eat one meal together, even if that meant Emma picked up takeout and took it to him at work because he couldn't get away.

"Dad," she told him, looking him in the eye. "I'm nearly twenty-five years old. I have no idea what it means to be parent."

Her father sighed. "Being a parent is both the simplest thing and the most complicated thing you'll ever have to go through," he told her. "It's simple in that: as a parent, the only thing you have to remember is that it's not about you anymore. It's complicated in that you are raising a little person who will become a member of this society which means you are responsible for their future."

"No pressure," Emma cracked, but she didn't feel the mirth radiating from the joke the way she normally would. She shook her head and ran her fingers through her hair.

"Emma," he told her. "Being a parent wasn't something I expected to happen to me as young as I was. I had just gotten married, I was still in law school, and I was focused on earning enough so we could start a family. But plans don't always work out the way you expect them to. A lot of the time, plans are completely detailed in favor of what's supposed to happen. And you were supposed to happen. And this baby..." He let his voice trail off and his eyes dropped to her stomach. "This baby is supposed to happen. You need to decide if you want to do this by yourself or if you want to involve Underwood."

Emma rubbed her lips together. "What do you think I should do?" she asked tentatively.

Her father sat back in his chair, shifting his weight to get comfortable. "I can't make that decision for you," he told her, his voice serious. "I can't tell you what to do. The only thing I can do is speak from experience. As a father, I would want to know. I know that even though you aren't saying it, you must be worried about him leaving you because you're pregnant. But lying to him isn't going to make him want to stay with you, either. If he leaves, it says more about him than it does about you. You will surprise yourself, you will surprise everyone,, my darling. You are stronger than you give yourself credit for. It may not be what you want to hear, but I want you to know that God would never put you in a situation He didn't think you couldn't handle." He wrapped his arm around her shoulder and squeezed. "Whatever you choose to do, I support you. But you wanted my opinion and I'm giving it to you."

Emma smile wryly at her father. "Yeah," she agreed, placing her head on his shoulder. "I know that. But that doesn't mean I'm still not scared of that he'll do what he what, I still hid this from him. And we fought about hiding stuff from each other before." She pressed her lips together. "I just don't like fighting with him."

Her father snorted. "Couples fight, Em," he told her. "They might not scream and yell, but everyone fights. Its a given in life. And that's the way it should be, or life would be boring. You just have to adapt to what works best for you and Kyle. And, now that there's a child involved, you have to remember that it's not about you guys anymore. For some people, this is easy. For others, not so much. Want to know why? Because one wants it to work, and one doesn't. One tries and one doesn't. You both have to want it and you both have to want to the same things. The whole opposites attract adage is bullshit. People also make mistakes. You have to decide if they're worth forgiving or not."

He cocked his head to the side. "What are you thinking right now?" he asked. "What's your plan?"

"I have my doctor's appointment next week," she murmured, dropping her eyes down at her hands. She twisted her fingers. Even though her father knew about the pregnancy, that didn't mean it still wasn't weird to be talking about it to him.

She wished...

No. She didn't wish for her mother. Emma didn't think she would ever be that desperate.

Still, she wished she had someone to talk to about what she was going through. Harper knew, sure. But Harper knew that Zachary Ryan was the one. If they got pregnant, Emma knew they would be elated. Harper wouldn't hesitate to tell Zach because she knew how he was going to react.

Emma sighed. She knew she needed to tell Kyle regardless of how he chose to respond. She just had no idea how to do it. And, more than that, she needed to figure out the appropriate time of when to do that. Because even if he was happy that they were going to have a baby together, that didn't fix their problems.

And if they were going to make this work, if they were going to go deeper than ever, they needed to sort out their issues.

"Okay," her father said, clapping his hands together and nodding curtly. "That's a good first step. Is anyone going with you?"

She knew what he was asking: was she going to tell Kyle and was she going to do it soon?

"I have no plans beyond that," she admitted before teasing her bottom lip with her teeth. She blinked, trying to clear her mind from the fog, from the overwhelm. "I've researched the first appointment and my book has suggested questions to ask the OBGYN but beyond that, I have no idea what to expect..." She let her voice trail off and looked back at her father. "Do you remember what your appointment was like?"

Her father paused, cocking his head to the side and rubbing his chin with his hand. "Things have changed so much in twenty-four years, Em," he told her. "I do remember that your mother wasn't afraid. When I told her I might not make it, she didn't get upset. She could do anything by herself. She was fiercely independent; it's why I fell for her in the first place. But I switched some things around and I went." He paused so he could look her in the eye. "We didn't plan you, Emma. But your mother was determined to see the pregnancy through no matter what. She ate healthy. She exercised - and let me tell you, your mother hated exercise. She wasn't afraid of being pregnant."

Emma snorted, rolling her eyes. "Just of being a mom," she muttered.

"No," her father said. "You're right. She was terrified of having someone depend entirely on her for everything."

Emma furrowed her brow and shot her father a look that requested he elaborate.

"Think about it, Em," he told her. "Having a child means you created a life. You are now responsible for sheltering it, protecting it, feeding it, clothing it. They are completely dependent on you to survive. She couldn't handle that responsibility. She did what she felt was required - breastfed you the first year but around the time you were three, she couldn't take it anymore and left." His eyes widened. "It wasn't your fault, though, Em. I hope you know -"

Emma held her hand up. "Dad," she said. "I know. But it still sucks knowing my mom couldn't handle being a mom." Without warning, she felt her eyes start to prick with tears - something she thought was impossible, considering how many tears she had already cried the past few days. "Knowing that it was so easy to leave me."

"It wasn't, honey," he told her, enveloping her into a tight hug. "I'm sure it wasn't. You have to remember she bonded with you in those three years. I... I'm not going to defend her actions. But let me tell you from personal experience, you are not easy to leave. And you're better than buying into that bullshit."

Warmth flooded through her system and she pulled her father into a tight hug, grateful that he was here with her.

Chapter 10

IT WAS the second game of the playoffs and all Emma could do was try to think about anything except the churning in her stomach. Morning sickness had hit her like a beast at all times of the day and right now, she could barely sit up straight let alone focus on the game. She still hadn't spoken to Kyle; she wanted to give him time. As much time as he needed. In fact, she wanted to ensure that he knew she supported him, regardless of whether there were issues between them or not.

She took great care to pull on clothes that were somewhat loose - something she didn't wear under normal circumstances. Her white jeans were already starting to feel snug and she wore a faded navy-blue boyfriend shirt with the Newport Beach Seagulls scrawled across her chest in white slanted text. She had on a matching hat that hid the top half of her face and left her hair down. As much as she wanted to pull her hair back, any pressure on the back of her head would cause a headache to breakout and that was the last thing she needed.

Currently, she was leaning forward, trying to ease the queasiness but trying not to make it obvious she was in any sort of discomfort. Despite the fact that her father knew about her current predicament didn't mean she wanted to revert back into a child and have him take care of her - even if that would make everything easy.

Right now, she needed to take care of herself.

"I'm actually surprised we got home ice advantage," her father murmured from behind her. "This team constantly surprises me. It's the best part about being a fan." He cocked a grin. "Seraphina Hanson's most recent press conference was one for the books, let me tell you what. Calling out Phil Bambridge like that. And then Bambridge had the nerve to release grainy photos of two people kissing, claiming it's Hanson and Thorpe. How freaking sexist, am I right? Seraphina isn't stupid enough to get involved with her best player." He snorted, rolling his eyes.

Emma pressed her lips together, trying to hide a smile. She trusted her father with *almost* anything. If he found out about Seraphina and Brandon Thorpe, Emma knew he wouldn't say anything but it might cause him to lose respect for her, and considering Seraphina was a friend of Emma's, she didn't want that to happen. And anyway, Emma knew that once Seraphina was ready to come out and tell everyone, she would.

Not that it was anyone's business.

"I hope this game goes well," he continued. His arms were crossed over his chest, his eyes on the players warming up. "The Sacramento Suns have always been a tough team and their fans are nearly as awful as the Hollywood Stars." He glanced over at his daughter. "You hungry? You're eating for two now."

"Actually," Emma said, her eyes still on Kyle even though she wanted nothing more than to look away. "I'm not eating for two until the second trimester."

From the corner of her eyes, she could see her father push up his brow.

"It's the truth," she continued. "It's one of the first things they tell you in the book. What the healthy amount of weight you should gain."

"And let me guess," he mumbled, raising a skeptical brow. "You're following the book diligently?"

Emma snorted. "I wish," she said. "It's difficult when all I'm craving is everything bad for you. Jalapeño poppers. Jalapeño cheeseburgers with extra special sauce. Spaghetti with tons of cheese. Cheese by itself. Lots and lots of cheese." She sighed wistfully, just thinking about cubed cheddar.

"Emma," her father said flatly. "I'm glad you bought the book and you're actually reading it. But I want you to know that you are entitled to indulge your cravings every once in a while."

"I know, Dad," she murmured.

He pressed his lips together. "Have you considered getting in touch with your mother about the whole thing?" he asked casually, looking away and at the glass.

"I haven't even told Kyle," she pointed out. "Why the hell would I tell the woman who walked out on me when I was three before I told the baby's father. Why would I tell her anything?"

"You don't have to," he said, turning to look at her. "That's not what I'm saying. She was around your age when she got pregnant. She might know how to handle it, or, at least, tell you what she went through. Granted, she wasn't as ambitious as you are, but a different perspective might help."

"Maybe," Emma allowed in a curt voice. "But not hers. Ever." She clenched her jaw and looked away, crossing her arms over her chest.

"You might have to," her father pointed out, his voice more curt than she expected from him. She gave him an odd look. "You have a responsibility to that child. Now, I'm not sure what you plan to do in terms of prenatal care. Going to your appointments, eating right, and taking a prenatal vitamin every day are great first steps. But what about prenatal screenings? What about planning for your baby's health insurance? One of the responsibilities you have to your baby is the health of the mother's family and the father's family. That means eventually telling

Kyle and getting his history. And it also means talking to your mother."

"But what about all the adopted men and women who don't have access to that?" Emma asked.

Her father cut her a look. "Em," he said. "Do you know how badly those adopted parents wish they had the opportunity to even communicate with the people who abandoned them - especially expecting couples? And you have the opportunity. You do. And you're taking it for granted."

"Just because I want that woman to stay out of my life does not make me selfish," Emma snapped. She realized she was in public and pressed her lips together, feeling slightly regretful for her outburst.

"At the very least, please think about it," he murmured.

"Why?" Emma asked, with more attitude than she originally intended. "Dad, no offense, but there's no way you're going to change my mind about this. This woman does not have the right to be in my life. She doesn't get to know my life. And she definitely does not get a place as a grandmother to my child." She cut her father a look, almost as if she couldn't believe the suggestion had come out of his mouth. "Why are you suddenly on her side? Last time I checked, she left me AND you, not just me."

Her father sighed and it was only in that moment did she realize just how tired and aged he looked. Even though he was in his fifties, he looked like he was in his early forties and had the energy to show for it. Emma always told him the next woman he ever got serious would not only have to keep up with him but realize just how lucky she was to have him.

Except, there was no other woman.

Sure, he dated but there was nothing serious. Emma never met any of them - something she was secretly glad about. If she didn't meet anyone, she wouldn't have to smile and pretend she was happy for her father when, in reality she was suspicious that this woman was nothing but a gold digger. But now, she realized it was selfish. Now, she realized she wished her father had found someone to make him happy because no one deserved a lifetime of loneliness.

"I'm over holding onto the resentment I had for her," her father explained slowly, pinching the bridge of his nose with his fingers. "I turned into an untrusting, bitter old man. I realized that I didn't want that to be my life. I refused to allow her to have that power over me. So I let it go and I've never been happier."

"So you aren't mad at Mom anymore?" Emma asked doubtfully with a raised brow. "You've forgiven her?"

Her father nodded once. "I have," he said with a nod.

Emma furrowed her brows. "Why would you do that for a woman who treated you like garbage?" she asked. She didn't understand how her father could be so zen after everything that had happened. "You told me that all couples fight and I need to figure out what I could forgive and what I couldn't." She narrowed her eyes. "Please tell me that what she did to us isn't so easily forgiven."

He sighed. Her breath caught in her throat.

"Emma," he told her. "I didn't forgive her for her. I did it for me."

"Don't use that self-help bullshit with me," she told him. Her voice was getting shrill; she couldn't help it. She hoped no one could overhear her, but she almost didn't care if they could.

"It's not self-help if it's the truth," he told her, still the everpatient father. She didn't think it was his intention but it almost sounded as though he was condescending, as though he was trying to humor her beliefs even though he had some knowledge that it wouldn't work out. Almost like he didn't take her seriously. "I decided for myself I wasn't going to allow her to control how I felt. I took back that control. I let it go. She no longer has a hold on me but, clearly, she still has a hold on you to the point where you don't even trust Kyle not to leave you. You think everyone is going to leave you."

He pressed his lips together, looking away. She could tell he was going to pull one of his lawyer tricks on her, get her with his words, perhaps manipulate her own so it proved his point. There was a reason he had a waiting list of clients who wanted to use his services. "There's a reason you don't share things with Kyle. There's a reason you can't even tell him you want to dance on Broadway. You're afraid. You're afraid because what if he doesn't support your dream? What if he doesn't want you to go? And normally, you wouldn't care but Kyle is different. You love Kyle. You love him with every fiber of your being and that scares you because now, you have something to lose. So you keep him at an arm's length because there's a little voice in the back of your head whispering terrible things and you believe that voice. You believe that voice because your mother left you. The one person who isn't supposed to leave. So if she left you, why the hell wouldn't Kyle?" He twisted in his seat and placed both hands on her shoulders. "Listen to me, Emma Winsor. You are not unlovable. You are worthy of love. You are worthy of a steady, safe, reliable relationship. You are worthy. Do you under-stand me?"

Without warning, Emma burst into silent tears. Somehow, her father said exactly what she needed to hear. She knew they were at the game, knew people were probably giving them odd looks, but she didn't care. She needed to feel his safe embrace as his words started to sink in. They were pretty and she knew he meant each one - not just because he was her father but because they were true.

Of course, it was easier said than done but she would start working at it. She needed to. She deserved as much.

"So," she said, trying to keep her voice down. Just because people saw her a certain way didn't mean they had to overhear their conversation. "What do I do, Dad? I can't just do this cold turkey. I can't change who I've been for the past twenty-four years over night. What do I do?"

"Honey, first and foremost, you need to figure out what you

want," he replied as they slowly broke apart. "Not what you think Kyle wants. Not what you think you should want. But what you really want out of life. Out of your relationship. Then, talk to Kyle and see if he wants the same things. And talk about it. Once you both get on the same page, it'll get easier."

She nodded, rubbing the back of her hands across her cheeks. "So you think I should talk to him?" she asked.

He nodded his head. "I do," he told her. "And soon. Now, let's watch the game and hope that Game 2 does better than the last one."

Emma leaned back in her chair, sniffling. Her eyes caught sight of the back of Kyle on the bench and her heart swelled. He was worth it. He was worth the risk.

Game 2 definitely was not better than Game 1, but Emma was going to talk to Kyle anyway.

Chapter 11

EMMA DIDN'T CARE about decorum. She didn't care if Kyle needed space or time; he had two days of that. She needed to apologize. She needed to make this right.

The game had been a disaster. The Suns beat them six to zero despite the home ice advantage. She hadn't seen a game played so poorly since their 2010-2011 season, where they came in under five hundred - which meant they didn't break even with the amount of games they played. That was when Ken Brown fired the coach and brought in Henry Wayne to coach. Things started turning around at that point; they never made the play-offs but at least they played better.

To be honest, Emma had no idea what she could do to tell Kyle she was sorry. She knew she needed to put herself out there but not in a way where it put him on the spot or made him uncomfortable. She kissed her father on the cheek once the game was over and headed into the team store to see if there was anything she could get for him.

Which was stupid since Kyle had everything he could want and wasn't particularly materialistic.

Her eye caught sight of an adorable polar bear with a

Newport Gulls home jersey on. She couldn't help but smile at it? And for a minute, she imagined it in the corner of an oak crib, keeping a sleeping baby company. On a whim, she decided to buy the bear, using her season ticket holder discount, and went down to the locker rooms to wait for Kyle to emerge from the locker room.

When she got there, Harper and Zach were just leaving.

"Em, what are you doing here?" Harper asked, furrowing her brow.

Emma tilted her head to the side. "I'm here to see Kyle," she said as though it was obvious.

Harper and Zach glanced at each other before Zach murmured, "Emma, he took off right after Cherney released us. I think he wanted to go home before the media asked to interview him."

"Oh." She felt her cheeks burn with frustration at the fact that they knew something she didn't about her boyfriend. She felt like an idiot, a fool. She was angry with Kyle for ditching her and angry with herself for causing this tension between them in the first place. "Okay, well, I'll check on him then."

"That's probably a good idea," Zach agreed with a nod. "He needs all the love he can get."

Emma pressed her lips together and looked away.

"Do you want us to walk with you to your car?" Harper asked, her voice soft and compassionate.

Emma looked at her friend and squeezed the bag holding the bear. She shook her head, forcing a smile on her face. "No," she said. "No, I'll be okay. Thank you, though."

Harper pressed her lips together and squeezed her forearm. "Call me when you're home," she murmured.

Emma nodded. She couldn't find it in her to respond.

She huffed a sigh and decided she could figure out what to do on her way to the car. She needed some space anyway, from everyone. She needed to figure out what was right for her - and for the baby. Telling Kyle had to be done, no matter what. She knew she needed to find the right time, of course. Being in the middle of a fight wasn't going to help the situation at all, considering she had kept something from him which started the original fight in the first place. He also might think she was lying in order to trap him in their relationship if he was contemplating leaving her after her idiotic mistakes.

She hoped not. She hoped not more than anything. Space, yes, fine, take as much space as he needed. But to break up?

Her eyes started to tear up and as she emerged from the elevator, she took a breath and tried to control herself. She needed to make sure she didn't look as wrecked a she felt.

Regardless of all of that, she had to tell him. Because he needed to know. He needed all of the information so he could make the right decision.

And she owed him that much.

By the time she reached her car, she knew she wanted to meet him at his place. She just hoped that he would be open to seeing her.

She parked in his driveway where she always parked, on the right side of the garage because he always parked on the left side inside his garage. She pressed her lips together and inhaled deeply, curling her fingers into fists and balling them up by her hips. She followed the paved pathway up to his front door and reached up to knock...

...before hesitating and slowly dropping her hand back down at her side.

Was this the right thing to do? Should she really be here?

He already had a rough night and considering all they had been through, she highly doubted she was the first person he even wanted to be.

"But this isn't about hockey," she mumbled to herself and placed a hand over her stomach. She couldn't even imagine something was actually growing inside of her body. Besides her new breasts, her morning sickness, and her emotions, she didn't feel pregnant. Sometimes, she actually forgot - as bad as that sounded.

But then her breasts would twinge or she would start tearing up at a car commercial or she would dash to the nearest toilet. Almost as though the baby was reminding her that it was there, deep inside her pelvis, waiting to meet her in the next nine months.

Kyle was going to find out eventually. Whether her raging hormones, her bigger boobs, or her belly, he would realize what was going on and their tiff from a couple of days ago would be nothing to what it would be.

"Courage," she whispered to herself. "Have courage."

She took another deep breath and this time, forced herself to knock on his front door without thinking about it.

It didn't take long before Kyle opened the door, his short blond hair damp, as though he had just gotten out of the shower. He wore a white thermal with the Gulls' logo across it - one of her favorite shirts on him. It fit him elegantly and she couldn't help but let her eyes linger on his broad shoulders, the stretch of the anchor across his broad chest. He wore faded blue jeans and socks on his feet. This was one of the outfits he wore if he knew he wasn't going out but didn't want to hang out in his pajamas all day - or night, considering.

"Hey." His crystal blue eyes seemed surprised to see her at his doorstep and she couldn't blame him. They never really fought before, but when things got tense, they gave each other a few days to get over it and when they saw each other again, they didn't talk about whatever was bothering them.

Emma only realized now that that probably not the healthiest way to handle problems.

"Hey," she told him, trying to sound casual and not upset that they hadn't spoken in the past couple of days. "Do you mind if I..." She let her voice trail off and gestured to the door, pushing up her brows.

"Yeah." He didn't even hesitate. That certainty in her was nearly her undoing.

After what she had done to him, how could he so easily forgive her?

Her father's voice floated in homer head. 'Because he loves you more than the mistake you made,' he told her. 'He loves you more than his pride. Do you think people want to be mad at each other? Of course they don't. They want their feelings heard, acknowledged - even if there is no agreement - and they want to figure out a compromise that works best for both of them.'

"What's up?" he asked, shoving his hands into his pocket as Emma shut and locked the door behind her.

She slowly turned around so they could lock eyes. She could see the pain and frustration in his eyes after that game and she wanted nothing more than to wrap her arms around him and pull him close so he was safe, so he knew that this what he was going through would pass. Until she realized that maybe, just maybe, she was the cause of his poor play. Maybe he could feel her withdraw on some subconscious level and he was worried about it. And instead of talking about the worry, it reflected in his play.

She gnawed at her bottom lip. She needed and fix this. She needed to fix this now.

"Before you say anything," he told her, "I've been running every morning for three miles. I'm trying to get into better shape."

Emma furrowed her brow. "You think this has anything to do with your play?" she asked, not unkindly. She pressed her lips together; she didn't want to simply react. She wanted to make sure she said the right thing, or at least, didn't allow her emotion to dictate her diction.

"This is about us. You and me."

"Oh."

Emma couldn't tell what that single word meant. She wasn't

sure if he was disappointed or wary or stiff or defensive or... She couldn't tell. Maybe it didn't matter. Maybe all that mattered was fixing this thing between them, removing the tension between them in whatever way she possibly could. Her head felt light. She started to feel dizzy but she pushed through her nervousness, ignoring her racing heart.

"First, I wanted to apologize," she said. "I should have told you about Broadway. I should have told you that because you deserve to know. I want to know all about you and I'm sure you want to know all about me. And I'm the one who's keeping up this wall between us because I'm afraid you're going to leave."

"Emma, I'm crazy about you," he told her. "I don't intend to leave you -"

"I know, I know," she said with a small smile, her cheeks flushing pink. "But it's still hard to wrap my mind around the forever portion of a serious relationship." She shook her head, trying to clear it. "My father has been my only constant in my life." She picked her eyes up to lock with him. "It's hard for me to trust that anyone else will stay."

"Em, I'm in it for the long haul," he told her. "Yeah, I want to talk to you about our future plans. I want to talk about trips and marriage and kids. Eventually. When you're ready."

She snapped her head in his direction. "You're ready?" she asked, pushing her brows up.

"I'm ready to start planning it," he told her. He shifted under her gaze and she realized she must have some sort of glare on her face, a judgmental look that indicated that he was crazy for even wanting to talk about it. Which wasn't going to fix things. It was her defensive mechanism jumping up to protect her when things got too serious.

Her heart started to race. She was getting lightheaded. Maybe this was too much, too soon to fix...

But no.

No.

She wanted to fix this. She needed to tell him.

"Kyle," she murmured. "I'm - I need to talk to you about something."

His eyes sharpened and there was concern pooling into the depth of blue. She wanted to take away that concern, wanted to push it off of his mind. But she couldn't. Because she wasn't quite sure how he was going to react.

"Okay," he told her, his voice a gentle mumble. "I'm ready to listen."

"It's..." She shook her head. Little dots blocked out a direct line of vision. She blinked, trying to get them to go away. "I'm not sure it's what you want to hear..."

"Tell me," he said, taking a step towards her. He furrowed his brow, cocking it to the side. "Emma... are you okay? You don't look so good."

"What?" Emma blinked but that was too much. She nearly tripped over something -

Except no. It wasn't there. Nothing was there.

That was strange.

As a dancer, she always had good balance. She never lost it for no reason.

And then, the dots turned bigger until her vision turned black and she fainted in that moment.

Chapter 12

KYLE PLAYED like shit and he didn't know why. This never happened to him. Not when he was a kid playing in a league. Not when he was a draft pick playing in the AHL. He always was on point, even if the team wasn't. He had fifty-two goals last season; he produced the most offense on the team the past three years. Now, his stats barely reflected he was actually part of the team. He was a minus the last four games due to the fact that goals had been scored against the Gulls while he was on the ice. He had gotten lazy; instead of skating after a player, he reached with his stick, which caused him to get stupid penalties. For whatever reason, their penalty kill was atrocious - they only managed to kill off thirty-seven percent of them during the regular season - and the trend seemed to be following them in the post-season, considering the last two home games were bad.

As in 4-1 and 6-3 bad.

The Sacramento Suns were not this good.

The Gulls were not this bad.

Hell, Kyle was not this bad.

He clenched his teeth and shook his head. The minute

Cherney and Thorpe released them after the game, Kyle bolted. He didn't want to talk to the media. He didn't want to talk to the guys. All he wanted was to be by himself and think. And yeah, that would probably make things worse considering he was his harshest critic but he couldn't sit around and pretend everything was fine when it wasn't. He wasn't like Zachary Ryan. He didn't have the energy to be charming - not that anyone ever considered him charming in the first place.

He also wanted to avoid Emma.

Granted, after their disagreement - a nice word for what happened between them - he wasn't even sure she would even show up at the locker room after the game like she normally did, but on the off-chance she did, he didn't want to be there.

He couldn't face her. Not yet.

His heart ached and he tried to force the feeling down, so deep he couldn't feel it anymore. He slid into the driveway of his relatively humble four-bedroom home in a quiet part of Newport Beach. He didn't want to live beach-front like some of the guys. He preferred the solitude, the stillness, of some of the neighborhoods. He locked his car before heading to the path that would take him to his front door. He had a black gate that he undid the latch to before clicking it back into place and then unlocked the front door before heading in and sliding off his jacket.

The first thing he intended to do was shower and get the sweat and stench of the game off of his body.

Then, after that...? Well, he didn't know. Normally, he would have cracked open a beer and slowly enjoyed it while allowing him to focus on everything but the game, everything but Emma.

Now?

He cut drinking out before the post-season, deciding that even though it wasn't a direct factor in his poor play didn't mean it was helpful to him. He hired a personal trainer who would help with his endurance as well as with his nutrition and was already making changes to his diet. Physically, he felt better in the last week than he did the last year. To be honest, he was surprised that it all went back to food and diet even though it seemed like common sense.

He shook his head, heading to the bathroom, stripping off his clothes and heading into the hot shower connected to his master bedroom. He lingered there longer than his usual ten minutes, feeling the beads of water run down his back, sweep over his skin. He was being cleansed. He was being rid of the negativity that lingered on his body.

He wanted to be rid of it all.

The shower soothed him. By the time he got out, he was relaxed, his mind clear and less distracted with hockey and Emma. He would flip on Netflix, maybe watch a mindless comedy show that would keep his thoughts at bay, prevent him from thinking too much and then getting tense all over again.

He was just about to crash on his leather couch and flip on his television when he heard the door knock. He furrowed his brow, dropping his towel and rifling through the hamper so he could quickly throw on something to wear.

Who the hell could possibly be bothering him right now? There was no way in hell the media even knew where he lived except Harper Crawford and there was no way she would go to his place just for a story. She wasn't like that. It could be one of his teammates but they knew him well enough to know when he stomped off, he wanted to be alone. Didn't want anyone to bother him about reassurance or worse - talking. Which left Emma. But that didn't make sense because Emma was angry with him. Wouldn't tell him important things he wanted to know like that she was applying to go to school in New York. That she one day dreamed of dancing on Broadway.

He clenched his teeth together at the thought. How could she not trust him with something as important as that - as a dream she had had since she was little. Those were things you shared with your significant other. At least, that was what Kyle thought.

'And have you shared everything with her?' a voice pointed out as he made his way to the front door. 'Every little detail about you. About what you want to be now, what you wanted to be when you were a kid?'

He pressed his lips together and looked through the peephole of the door, refusing to answer his own question.

He furrowed his brow when he saw Emma standing there on his doorstep, looking ridiculously beautiful in all of her uncertainty. Her hazel eyes were looking to the left, her blonde bangs nearly grazing her eyelashes. She seemed... uncomfortable wasn't the right word. Hesitant, perhaps. Almost as though she wasn't sure if she should be here. But she showed up anyway.

Kyle felt his heart squeeze together. He hadn't realized how much he missed Emma until he saw her standing there, bathed in the shadows of the darkness, glowing in his porch light. He didn't like that she shifted, that she doubted he would answer. Then again, he couldn't exactly blame her. They hadn't spoken since their tiff a few nights ago and it sucked. He hated being apart from her. He hated not being near her. Even when he was on the ice, focusing on the game, he felt a sense of safety knowing she was under the same roof as he was, knowing that she was with him, supporting him, no matter what happened, and would continue to show up regardless. During the commercial stoppages of the game, he would catch her from the corner of his eye, watching him or talking to her father. It made him feel special, knowing she was here for him. He never told her this, didn't like to reveal something that made him vulnerable, but it was true. She didn't realize it, but she gave him strength. Gave him a strength he hadn't realized existed within himself.

He didn't know how to live without it.

But at the same time, if she couldn't give him herself fully and wholly, he couldn't commit to being with her. It would absolutely break his heart but he knew it was the right thing.

Now, though, she was standing outside his porch and perhaps that meant something.

Kyle didn't hesitate letting her in. When she walked by him, she smelt like some floral scent mixed with vanilla. He thought it was lavender; at least, that was what he remembered her wearing him before their first Christmas. In case he had wanted to get her some lotion or perfume.

He ended up buying her a beautiful necklace and reserving a day at the Grand Californian spa - a Disneyland hotel that had one of the best spas Kyle could remember. He also got her twelve different lotion-body spray combinations, thanks to the help of a sales associate from Bath and Body Works.

He was pretty proud of himself that Christmas.

"Hey."

He inwardly cursed himself for the lame greeting he gave her, rolling his eyes internally. He felt his body stiffen in her presence, always on his guard because he wasn't sure what to expect from her. Not necessarily that that was a bad thing but he felt as though she kept him at an arm's length away from him because...

He didn't know. He didn't know why she was guarded with him at times.

"Hey," she told him, picking up her eyes and locking them with his.

Damn her penetrating gold-green eyes. He could never look away, no matter how hard he tried.

He was an idiot.

He assumed she was here to talk about his play.

He had no idea why he would assume that. Maybe it was his own way of keeping her at a distance, to keep his guard up around her. The hurt that flashed in her eyes based on that assumption was enough to curse his name.

Of course, he didn't show her that. He wouldn't reveal that part of himself just yet, not when he still wasn't sure where they stood. This whole thing was stupid, completely and utterly stupid. All he wanted to do was pull her in his arms and kiss her mouth with passion and fierceness. His body ached to be inside of her once again, to feel her writhe and move underneath him. To feel her slickness mold to his cock, to see her face turn up with ecstasy - ecstasy he was giving her and no other man could.

Was it wrong to think about sex now?

Maybe it was because he hadn't had it in the past few days and just smelling that flowery vanilla was making him remember her body's natural musk as it wafted over him when he was on top of her, surrounded his senses and put him under a spell as they were wrapped up in each other.

He suppressed a shudder and managed to focus on what she was saying. And what she said was astounding, something he didn't quite believe he would ever hear from her: an apology. An explanation.

And then, something happened. Something that caused his heart to stop. Her eyes fluttered before rolling in the back of her head and her entire body dropped to the floor. It was a hard thump; he knew she was unconscious.

But why?

No time for that. He immediately called nine-one-one. He probably could have taken her to the hospital himself but he wasn't sure if she should be moved or what he should do except let the medical professionals handle it.

After that, he called Emma's father to let him know what was going on and to ask what hospital he should route the ambulance to. He couldn't believe he didn't know her health care provider. He should know this. He was her goddamn boyfriend, for crying out loud.

The fire fighters arrived in the next five minutes. Kyle explained that she had been talking and then just dropped. They checked her vitals before moving her into the ambulance. Kyle climbed in after them.

"Looks like a simple case of dehydration," one of them

murmured to Kyle while keeping his eyes on Emma's uncon-scious frame.

He didn't care. All he knew was Emma was on the floor and he couldn't help her. All he wanted to do was help her.

"She's going to be okay," one of the fireman told him.

That did little to reassure him.

Chapter 13

HER HEAD HURT.

Why did her head hurt so badly?

She furrowed her brow, which only made it worse, and tried cracking open an eye but it was too bright, too much for her.

"Emma?" a familiar, tentative voice asked.

She wanted to open her eyes. She wanted to see if it was really him. But she couldn't. It was too bright.

"K-Kyle?" she managed to say. Her throat was scratchy and she could taste how bad her breath was, causing her to grimace.

Her head hurt. God, it hurt.

"Yeah, I'm here, Em," he murmured, walking over to her - she could hear his footsteps on the tile before she felt his hands take hers. They were cool and clammy, the kind of hands one had when someone was nervous, or worried.

"What's wrong?" she asked, tilting his head to the side. "Is everything okay?"

"Emma, do you know where you are?" another voice asked.

She furrowed her brow even further. "Dad?" she asked. "What are you doing here?"

"Kyle called me," he told her. She tried cracking open her

eyes and still couldn't keep them open. At least it wasn't as bright as before. "You fainted."

Upon hearing that, her eyes sprung open despite the pain. She immediately locked onto Kyle, standing there in what he was wearing when she had been over at his place. Which was...

Where was she? The beeping. The goosebumps on her arms. The scratchy material on her skin.

She was in a hospital.

Why was she in a -

"Is-" she asked, her wide eyes snapping into her father's.

He nodded, not needing any further explanation than that. Kyle glanced between them, an arched brow on his face, but he didn't ask what he clearly wanted to know: what was going on and what were they referring to?

Which meant he didn't know.

The doctor hadn't told him anything.

"What happened?" she asked, trying to sit up but feeling a flash of dizziness overtake her senses.

"Easy," Kyle murmured, instantly at her side, trying to ease her back down to her former position. "They're trying to hydrate you right now." He nodded at the IV attached to Emma's right arm. She must have been out to not feel the needle break through her skin. She always had a thing about needles.

"The doctor says you're dehydrated," her father said, raising a brow. Emma read his look easily. She glanced away, looking out the window so she wouldn't have to make eye contact with him.

"Which I don't understand because you're always on your students about keeping hydrated," Kyle said, slowly raising a critical brow. He crossed his arms over his chest and cocked his head to the side, waiting for an answer. "You get on my case about drinking enough during the game."

"I..." She let her voice trail off, ignoring the wrinkled brow and the crossed arms and the look currently occupying her father's face. "I guess I've had a lot of things on my mind. And I just... forgot.... to hydrate."

It sounded like bullshit even to her.

Kyle looked like he didn't believe her and was going to push further on the matter when her father cleared his throat, interrupting him. "Do you need something to drink?" he asked. "I know the doctors are getting fluids into your system but you sound..." He pointed to his throat. "Your throat sounds raspy."

"Yeah," she said, shifting her eyes to Kyle. "Would you mind getting me some water, Kyle?"

Kyle seemed surprised that he was the one who had been dismissed but nodded his head regardless. "Sure," he said, his arms still crossed over his chest. It was only then did she realize he was still wearing that thermal, that shirt that made him look even more beautiful to her than he already was. He shook his head and she could tell he wanted to say something, but he kept it to himself. Instead, he walked to the door, softly asking if her father wanted anything. When her father replied in the negative, he was gone.

"He still doesn't know, Em?" her father asked the minute the door was securely shut. "I thought you were going to tell him!"

"I was going to!" Emma exclaimed. She realized how loud and shrill her voice sounded and she winced, looking at the door, as though Kyle was going to walk right in at that moment and somehow know everything. Which made no sense. She rubbed her dry lips together. "It's why I went over to his place in the first place. You were right. We needed to fix everything. Having a baby isn't going to make things right, especially not with the issues between us. I wanted to clear up those issues first because we have those issues whether or not I'm pregnant."

"Yes." He placed his hand on his forehead, as though he had a headache and needed some respite for it. "Yes. That's good, Emma. But the boy is worried out of his mind about you. You should have seen him. He was frantic on the phone with me and he wouldn't sleep last night in your room. He refused to leave until just now, not to get any food, not to make a phone call. He has to board a plane tomorrow for game 3 up in Sacramento. But he's not going to be able to concentrate because he's worried about you."

"You're telling me that this whole thing is my fault?" Emma asked, her face completely aghast that her father would even say such a thing.

"Honestly, Emma?" her father said, raising his brow. "You need to take care of yourself. And your baby. And you're worried more about how Kyle is going to react than you do about how this could affect your dancing, the stress you're putting on yourself, on Kyle's play. Do what's responsible. You're afraid to talk to your mom because you don't want to deal with her even though it would benefit the baby and help your pregnancy."

Emma pressed her lips together and looked away. She wouldn't comment on that; she couldn't. What could she possibly say? He was right. She was being selfish because she didn't want to talk to her mother. And who had the potential to suffer because of it? Not Emma. Emma could care less.

The baby.

This baby that grew inside of her.

She clenched her teeth together but forced herself to look back at her father. He continued to stare at her, unwavering in his gaze. She nearly flinched underneath it but refrained from doing so.

Instead, she cleared her throat and forced herself to say, "Okay."

His brows perked at the word. "Okay?" he said with surprise. "Okay? What does that mean, okay?"

Emma furrowed her brow. "It means you're right," she told him, not bothering to keep the crankiness out of her tone. Her head still throbbed and her throat was raw and scratchy. "It means when I get out of here, I'd like you to give me her phone number so I can reach out to her and figure this out. It means I get what you're saying."

"Oh." He seemed surprised by her admittance to that and cocked his head to the side, crossing his arms over his chest. "Okay. I... I think that's a great idea, Em. I know how hard this must be for you."

She shook her head. "No you don't," she told him. "Dad, partners leave. Teams fall apart. It's no surprise marriages and partnerships and relationships would do the same thing. But you're not supposed to leave your children. You're not." Without realizing what she was doing, she placed a hand over her stomach. "And now, I have to go to her because I need something from her - the only thing I need that's going to benefit my child. And I'm going to do it for my child. Because she deserves it."

Her father quirked a brow. "She?" he inquired, a teasing smile on his face.

Emma shrugged. "It's just a gut feeling I have," she said. "Be careful, Dad. The females might soon outnumber you."

"Hon, you outnumbered me when it was just you," he said, his tone sardonic.

"So," she said, glancing around the hospital room. "Where do you think Kyle is? He's been gone for a while."

"Probably because I sent him to the cafeteria, telling him what comforted you the most was Fiji water," he said.

"I don't think they have Fiji water," she told him.

Her father smirked. "Exactly," he said. "Buys us more time to talk."

"How did you know he would leave just to get me Fiji water?" Emma asked, quirking a brow. It was a gentle gesture that didn't hurt her head too much.

"Please," he said with a snort, rolling his eyes. "Anyone can see that the boy is clearly crazy about you. Especially since you were hospitalized, he would want to do all he could in order to ensure you were comfortable." He paused a minute. "Don't take that for granted, Em. Not many people would drop everything for their partner, even in time of need."

Emma chewed her bottom lip, taking what he had to say into consideration. Her eyes were glassy but were not filled with tears. If they had been, it would have been easy to not let them fall.

"I've taken him for granted, haven't I?" she asked in a quiet voice.

Her father cleared his threat and looked away, which said enough. This wasn't what Emma wanted to hear but she couldn't help but listen. Maybe it wasn't what she wanted but it was what she needed. Kyle was a once in a lifetime guy and it wasn't just because of the fact that he played hockey profession-ally or had a sizable cock that fit her like a puzzle piece.

It was more than that.

He was a good man who treated her with respect and let her dictate the nature of their relationship. If she kept her guard up, he didn't push. If she started talking to him about private things, he listened. He stayed with her when she pushed him away, patiently waiting for the moment when she changed her mind and took him back in her arms. He knew she wasn't giving him her all and yet... and yet, he still stayed.

And that made no sense to Emma because no one deserved that treatment in a committed relationship. Especially not him.

"I tried making it right," she told him, "and then this whole mess happened."

At that moment, the doctor walked in wearing a typical lab coat and a friendly smile on his face. "Looks like you had quite the scare, Ms. Winsor," he said, glancing at her chart for confir-mation of her name. "How are you feeling?"

"Better," Emma agreed with a nod, slowly trying to push herself into a sitting position.

"Easy," the doctor said, gently placing his hand on her shoulder and easing her back to her position on the bed. "You need to rest. We're hydrating you right now with fluids but you need to make sure that you drink at least sixty-four ounces of water every day in your condition. The baby has started to hoard some of your liquid so you need to drink enough for both you and it."

"Baby?" a voice said at the door.

Emma's eyes shot to Kyle, who was standing there with a bag of three large Fiji waters, his eyes wide, his skin unnaturally pale. She looked to her father who glared at the doctor who had his own mouth dropping open, surprised.

"You haven't told him?" the doctor asked. "Perhaps I should leave you two alone."

"I guess so," she muttered under her breath.

Her father and the doctor stepped out, leaving Emma alone with Kyle.

Chapter 14

EMMA WATCHED Kyle from her bed in her hospital room. His hands were shoved in his pockets and his entire body was tense. But the look on his face wasn't angry. If she had to define it, she would say it was... contemplative.

"You're pregnant." His voice was flat but there was a touch of disbelief in it, as though he couldn't quite believe it. As though it was hard for him to wrap his mind around the concept. This, of course, didn't tell her if that was a good thing or a bad thing. It didn't reveal how he felt about this. The fact that he was still here after finding out about it was a big deal to her, though. That could only be a good sign.

Right?

"Yes," she said with a tight nod. She wanted to look at him but he wasn't looking at her and she didn't want to stare at him when he was occupied elsewhere.

"How long?" he asked, reaching up to cup the back of his neck with his hand.

"I'll be six weeks and four days today," she said. "If you mean how long have I known, I've known the past week. I think it happened when we were in Vegas. If you're asking how long until the baby comes, we're due November ninth."

"So you're keeping it?" he asked, locking eyes with her. "The baby?"

The word sounded so foreign in his mouth. Strange. Like even he didn't know what it meant let alone how to say it.

"I -" She was going to say she didn't know. But that would be a lie. And if she wanted things to be better between her and Kyle, she needed to be upfront and honest. She bit her lip from saying anything else and then nodded her head. "Yes. I am." She pressed her lips together. "I know we need to talk about all of this. I'm just not sure where to start."

"Let's start at the beginning," Kyle said as though it was the obvious thing in the world. He reached for the chair at her bedside but then thought better of it and continued to pace up and down the small room. "Where do you see us in a year, Em? In five years? In ten? Because I love being with you. But I can't half-ass relationships. It's why I've avoided them for so long. I've never found anyone worth my time. If I'm in, I'm all in. I want the vacations in the off-season. I want marriage. And yeah, I want a few kids."

Her brow pushed up, surprise on her face. "A few?" she asked.

He nodded. "A few," he told her with certainty. "And I want them with you, Emma. And I know we didn't exactly plan for this child but I'm really looking forward to raising it with you." He stopped pacing and threw her a tentative look, something out of character for him. He was always good at being confident - or, at least, appearing that way. "If that's what you want. I don't want to make you feel uncomfortable or force you to do something you don't want to do."

"Kyle," she told him. Her eyes were filling up with tears and she cursed this new ability to cry at every damn thing. "Of course I want you to do this with me. I-I don't know if I'd be able to do it alone."

Kyle gave her a disbelieving look. "You're stronger than you realize, Emma," he told her, as though it was the most obvious thing in the world. "The first six months of our relationship, I was paranoid that you were going to leave me because I know I'm not good enough for you. I am nowhere in your league. You're intelligent, beautiful, and graceful. And the crazy thing is, you don't even know it. You have this crazy fear that you aren't good enough, but the fact of the matter is, you're perfect just the way you are. You don't have to try and be the perfect girlfriend because you already are." He reached up to cup the back of his neck. "Honestly, I wished we talked more. Not just about hockey or dance but about us. I want to be more romantic but I worry because you don't really seem that much into it. I want to buy you flowers for no reason and go out to dinner and fancy restaurants. I've wanted to take you home to my family after a week of being together. I want to know what you're afraid of. I want to know more about your mom and what she did to you - just so I can hold you in my arms while you tell me, so you know I'm never ever going to leave. Not now. Not ever."

Emma pressed her lips together, trying to contain her tears. She hated crying. She didn't want to cry in front of Kyle. She didn't think she ever had and she didn't want to start now. But there was no stopping the tears from eclipsing her cheeks.

"Okay," she said with a small nod. "Okay."

His lips curled up. "Okay," he agreed with a nod. "So now what?"

"What do you mean?" she asked, tilting her head to the side, causing the tears to run down her cheeks. Kyle stepped over to her so he could wipe her tears away.

"Do we stay the way we are?" he asked, kneeling down so he was roughly level with her from her position on the hospital bed. "Do I propose? Do we move in together? What's the next step? I've never done this before."

Emma snorted. "I haven't, either," she said, looking with wide brown eyes. "I don't want you to marry me because I'm having your child, Kyle. I want to marry you because we want to be with each other for the rest of our lives."

"Do you honestly think I'd propose if I didn't want to be with you?" he asked raising his brows.

"I think you're notorious at doing the right thing," she told him, a small smile on her lips. "No matter what that is."

He pressed his lips together, biting back and smile that would have eclipsed his face and taken her breath away. He always did that, always seemed to prevent himself from showing when he was happy, but she could read him easily.

"That may be," he told her, "but I'm serious."

"I know," she agreed with a nod. "And you have no idea how much I appreciate that, Kyle. But I don't want this pregnancy to be the reason why you proposed to me. If you want to marry me in the future, I'm open to it. But I promised myself I would never let something else be the reason why I was stuck to someone for the rest of my life. Whether it's kids or history or... I don't know. And I don't want to put you in that same position." Kyle opened his mouth to say something but Emma interrupted, reading him clearly. "I'm not saying you don't want to marry me. I'm not saying that at all. But I want you to ask me because you've been planning to ask me or because the moonlight in my eyes just moves you or because the fireworks are going off at Disneyland. Not because you just found out we're going to have a kid together."

Kyle pressed his lips together to keep from saying anything. He seemed to take her words into consideration before nodding his head. He picked up his eyes to look at her and she saw the understanding in his sky blue eyes.

"I get it," he said, "but I do want to be part of this, Em. I want to be the one to hold your hair up while your puking in the toilet because of morning sickness. I want to watch as your boobs grow the size of melons. I want to run your aching feet and rub cocoa butter on your belly so you don't get stretch marks."

"Stretch marks are genetic more than anything," Emma pointed out.

"Well, I'll love you no matter what," he said, waving the thought away. "I don't want to miss a minute of it."

"That's good, Kyle," she told him, "because morning sickness has definitely hit me and it doesn't come just in the mornings."

"So..." He pressed his brows together. "How can I be part of this?"

Emma tilted her head to the side. "What, exactly, are you asking, Kyle?" she asked, unsure.

"If moving in is too much," he began hastily, his cheeks turning red. He couldn't look at Emma, which Emma found completely endearing. "Maybe you could stay over a few nights a week. When the baby is born, I would hope that you would consider moving in..." He shook his head. "I feel this is coming out wrong."

"Em." He picked his eyes up so they locked with hers and she could easily read the sincerity in the sky blue irises. "I've wanted you to move in after our first six months together. I just didn't want to bring it up because we hadn't talked about it and I didn't want to make you feel uncomfortable. If you had told me to wait six months to have sex with you, I would have. Because you're worth it to me. If you told me you just weren't looking for a serious relationship, I would take what I could get until I couldn't take it anymore." His blue eyes flashed into hers, his long fingers curling into fists. "I'm at the point where I can't take it anymore, Em. Something about us, about this -" he gestured between them, stopping his pacing so he could face her in order to emphasize his point - "it has to change. I want it to change - I *need* it to change. But I can't force you to change how you feel about me."

"You don't have to," she told him. "I promise, you don't. Kyle, I'm crazy about you, too. I've pushed you away because I'm afraid you'll leave. I know you've given me no reason to think that way but I'm being honest." She looked away, taking a breath. "My mom left when I was three. I've told you this. And I told you it didn't matter, that I had moved on, but the truth it, I'm not over it. I don't think I've ever gotten over it even though I think I have. And it's an issue I'm going to struggle with for a very long time. The only constant in my life is my dad. That's the way it's always been. Even my college friends and I have grown apart just because that's the natural progression of life. I don't want that to happen to me and you, Kyle."

"But pushing me away isn't going to help either," he pointed out. "I want to be there for you, Emma. I want to prove that I'm not like your mother or your friends or your ex-boyfriends. I'm going to stay. And I would stay, whether or not you're pregnant. But you have to be willing to give me that chance."

Emma nodded and Kyle stepped to the side of her bed so he looked over her.

"I know," she told him. "I know." She pressed her lips together. "I don't know how I feel about moving in right away. This pregnancy is a huge change in my life and it's something I'm still getting used to. But..." She rolled her eyes up to meet his. "But I'm open to it. I need that to be enough. For now."

Kyle rubbed his lips together and nodded his head. "It is," he told her. "I need to know that we'll be honest and upfront with things from now on. No matter what, we need to be able to trust each other."

"You're right," Emma agreed. "I'm sorry for hiding things. For Broadway. I just..."

"I know," he said. "I felt that way about telling people about my hockey aspirations." He placed a soft kiss on her forehead. "We're in this together now."

Chapter 15

WHEN SHE RELEASED from the hospital, she was told to see her OBGYN at her scheduled appointment the next day. Kyle should have been flying out with the team to Sacramento. Instead, he was sitting in the lobby with Emma, holding her hand and trying to keep the nervousness off of his face.

Seraphina had been extremely understanding. When he called her and asked for an emergency meeting that day, she rearranged her schedule to accommodate him. He left the hospital, promising Emma he would be back as soon as he was able and headed straight for Sea Side Ice Palace on Pacific Coast Highway, just across the street from the ocean. It was relatively empty save for a handful of cars parked in front of the team store, probably fans stocking up on playoff gear, considering it was the first time in their history that they had made playoffs.

Kyle parked close to the west club level entrance, which gave him quick access to an elevator that would take him to the administrative floor and right to Seraphina office.

As usual, her door was open and she was typing something

up on her computer. When she saw Kyle lingering in the door-way, she stood and gestured at a chair in front of her.

"Hey Kyle," she said with a smile. "Please come in. Have a seat." She waited for him to do so before she slid back into hers. "What brings you in today?"

Kyle released a breath he hadn't realized he had been holding in. He didn't know why but he assumed she was going to ask about his play, talk to him about everything he did wrong, and give him tips on what to do to make it right. Instead, she leaned back in her chair and kept a warm, open face that made him let down his guard slightly. Like he could trust her just a little bit.

"I know I'm scheduled to be on a plane in two hours," Kyle said, "but Emma is pregnant."

Seraphina's brows shot straight up her forehead. "That's... wonderful?" She smiled but tilted her head to the side. "This is probably going to come out the wrong way but this is a good thing, right? You guys wanted this?"

"We didn't exactly plan it," Kyle replied honestly, "but I'm..." He felt himself smile, which felt strange and unnatural. He wasn't much of a smiler; not that he didn't enjoy his job or wasn't happy in life. He just wasn't compelled to smile all the time. Until now. Until Emma, really. "I'm excited."

Seraphina beamed. "I'm glad," she told him. "You guys deserve it. How's Emma doing?"

"She's fine," he said. "There was a scare, though. I mean, she fainted because she was dehydrated. Everything's fine. The baby's fine. But her first doctor's appointment is tomorrow. And I want to be there."

"Of course, of course," Seraphina said with a nod, leaning forward and interlacing her fingers together, placing them on the surface of the desk. "Absolutely, you should be there. This is a big deal, Kyle. I do want you to know that people will say that we've benched you - made you a healthy scratch..."

"I don't care what they say about me," he muttered, his

hands on his jean-clad thighs. "They've written about you and said worse things. You've managed to survive."

Seraphina shrugged her shoulders and nodded her head. "I suppose that's true," she said. "The difference being I'm a woman and they think they have a right to say nasty things about me while you're a player and they only write shit when you aren't playing up to their expectations."

Kyle nodded. "I know what's being said about me," he muttered, crossing his arms over his chest and meeting her eyes. "I had a fifty-two goal season last year - somehow, I still didn't get the freaking Hart Trophy. That's beside the point..." He shook his head. "I can be on top of my game for the eighty-two season games we play but I have two below-average games and suddenly they're talking about how I'm a waste of cap space, who would take my contract in a trade, that sort of nonsense." He shook his head and snorted. "I know it's part of the game. I get it. But it's not like I don't know I haven't been playing up to my standards, either."

Seraphina pressed her lips together. "Not to get all psychology 101 on you," she said, "but do you have any idea why you've been distracted lately. Is it because of the pregnancy?"

"I didn't find out until yesterday," he explained. "I have no idea why I've been playing the way I've been playing. I think..." He shook his head. "Emma and I weren't getting anywhere. Trust me, I want her. I want to be with her for the rest of my life. But she was holding back and I..." He sighed. "I can't hold back when it comes to the people I care about. But I also wanted to respect her boundaries and not push her to get more intimate than what she was ready for."

"Yeah," Seraphina murmured. "I've noticed Emma is pretty reserved. But that's not necessarily a bad thing."

"No, I know," Kyle agreed. "I guess I just didn't realize it had been weighing on me for this long. And I think it finally manifested itself in my play."

"But you worked it out," Seraphina pushed, raising her brow.

Kyle nodded. "We obviously have a lot more to get through," he replied. "It's not going to happen overnight. But that's okay. Because being with Emma is worth it. The struggles we're going to face, the comments people are going to make, we'll deal with it.

He paused, and tilted his head to the side. "How are you holding up? With the whole Phil Bambridge thing?"

Seraphina's lips cocked into a smirk and she leaned back in her chair looking like a cat who had caught the canary. "Well, you do know he released those photos of two people who are kissing, claiming them to be me and Brandon Thorpe, right?" she asked.

Kyle felt his own lips tug up simply because of her tone and the amusement flashing in her blue-gold eyes. "Of course," he said. "Bambridge won't shut up about you and rumor has it the owners of the Blackjacks are going to fire him any second."

Seraphina nodded. "I almost feel bad about that," she told him. "Almost. But then he opens his mouth in front of the media and says something else incredibly offensive, incredibly stupid, and then I don't feel so bad anymore." She shrugged. "Bambridge is actually the last thing on my mind. Right now, we're down two games and we're going into Sacramento's building. I'm more concerned about passing the first round of the playoffs without any other controversies coming to bite us in the ass." She leaned forward, pressing up her brows. "People hate us, Kyle. They don't think we're good enough to be where we are. They think we're a dirty team who fought and pushed and kicked and screamed into a seeded spot who miraculously won home ice advantage. And we are." She furrowed her brow. "Were gritty but we're not dirty. The refs have an inherent bias against west coast teams." She rolled her eyes and Kyle had to smother a laugh. "Anyway, don't quote me on that because I don't want some ridiculous fine for telling the truth." She interlaced her fingers and moved her body she rested her arms on the surface of her desk. "Kyle, I know you probably have tons of stuff running through your head. You're going to be a dad. That's crazy and amazing and scary! And your team is in the playoffs for the first time in its twenty-year history. That's crazy and amazing and scary, too! But I need one thing from you."

Kyle nodded his head. "Name it," he replied.

"Take as much time as you need for Emma and you and this baby," she said, her eyes serious. "We support you no matter what. I don't want you to feel pressure to return to the game if you aren't ready." She pressed her brows up. "But when you are here, I need your focus. I need you here one-hundred percent of the time."

"No, I understand," Kyle said with a nod. "I'm sorry my head hasn't -"

Seraphina put her hand up in order to cut him off. "I know you have a lot going on," she said. "I respect that. I sympathize. Don't take this the wrong way but as your boss, I don't care. As your friend, I do. But you're an adult. An adult who now needs to figure out his commitments, prioritize them, and let us know. We're here to support you but I have no sympathy for martyrs." She furrowed her brow gently. "Do you understand?"

Kyle nodded his head. "Yes," he said, standing up. He stuck his hand out and Seraphina slid gracefully into a standing position and shook it. "I understand. Thank you."

Seraphina nodded. "Any time," she told him. "Now, get your shit together and congratulations."

Kyle couldn't contain the small grin on his face if he tried.

"WHAT ARE YOU DOING HERE, KYLE?" Emma asked as she watched him make her way over to her in the somewhat empty lobby of the third floor of the Kaiser Building.

"I'm here to support you," he told her, taking a seat before placing his hand over her stomach. "Both of you."

Emma grinned, though it was rather strained on her face. "I appreciate it," she said. "We both do. But you have to get to John Wayne to catch a flight in the next half hour. I'm early for the appointment and if you're with me, you won't catch your flight."

Kyle shrugged, wrapping his arm around her shoulders and tugging her closer to him. "I've already talked to Seraphina," he told her. "I think a break would do me good and help refocus my mind."

"No."

He furrowed his brow. "What do you mean, no?" he asked her.

"I mean, you have a team that needs you," Emma told him, a determined glint in her hazel eyes. "I am and I've always been a strong, independent woman who respects your travel job and trusts you implicitly. I can handle this on my own. And I will video tape everything. Everything. Or, if there's wifi on the plane, we can skype during the appointment so you won't miss anything. But you will miss the most important game of your career if you don't show up."

"And what makes you think this game is my most important?" he asked.

"Because," she said as though it was the most obvious thing in the world, "this is the game where you get your head out of your ass and you start playing the way you've been playing this whole season. This is the game where you start earning the Hart trophy. But it won't happen if you're here."

"But what if I want to be here?" he asked, though his voice wavered.

She nearly smirked. She had him.

"Kyle," she said, leaning toward him. "With me, you can have both." She nodded toward the door. "They need you more than I do right now. Trust me, when I'm giving birth, I will require your presence but right now, go. Be with your team. I'll be right here waiting for you." She placed her hand over her stomach. "We both will."

Kyle hesitated another moment and then placed a long, lingering kiss on her lips.

"I love you," he told her when he broke apart. "More than you'll ever know...." And with that, he took off.

Chapter 16

EMMA WANTED to get this over with.

Kyle texted her a few hours ago, informing her the plane had just landed. Her father was ordering pizza and chicken wings, having invited a couple of co-workers over to his place for game three. And Emma was sitting at an outdoor cafe in Lake Forest, waiting for her mother to show up.

After her appointment - where she was surprised she reared up when she heard the heartbeat of the child growing in her stomach - she sent Kyle the recording, knowing he probably wouldn't get to it for another couple of hours. It was absolutely astounding, seeing that little blob with the vibrating heart beat and in nine months, it was going to turn into a living, breathing human child. She couldn't believe it even though it was science. Even though - if everything lined up the right way - that was how biology worked.

It was still hard to remember that she was pregnant - except during the moments when she was hacking up her stomach, usually some time during the evening. Her stomach was still flat and from what she read, it probably would stay that way for the next three to four months. She had talked to her doctor about dancing, and while Emma had to amend certain moves - especially those that involved twisting her stomach - she was clear to dance during her pregnancy as long as she felt good.

She wanted to watch the game on time. She needed this meeting to hurry up. She didn't even want to be here. Without thinking about it, she placed her hand over her stomach. She was here for her baby. She had to keep reminding herself this but when she did, she relaxed as much as she could.

She called her dad who called Justin to get the number. Emma was the one who called; her father all but forced her, citing the fact that she was an adult and needed to handle things on her own.

When her mother answered, she sounded like a stranger. There was a hesitant warmth in her voice that did absolutely nothing for Emma. She didn't feel guilty for hating her mother; she didn't feel a sense of longing at having missed so much with her mother. She felt... nothing at all. In a way, that was reassuring. The thing was, Emma was worried that when she saw her mother again, she would immediately forgive her and forget about the years they hadn't shared together. And that was the last thing Emma wanted. She didn't want to forget. She didn't want her mother in her life anymore, even if she needed her now.

"Don't immediately turn her down," her father insisted. "Just give her a chance to explain her side. If you don't agree with it, fine. But don't shut the door without really knowing."

She wanted to ignore her father's advice. She didn't want to give her mother any chance in hell to possibly come back to her life. But he made sense.

As much as she hated to admit it, he was right. Her mother was going to be her child's grandmother who wanted to be part of their lives. Why would Emma prevent that from happening? It wasn't her child's fault that her mother left, just like it wasn't Emma's.

"Emma."

Emma tensed when she heard the sound of the voice. Somehow, it was both familiar and strange at the same time. She recognized it but then she didn't. It was an odd sensation, like her past crept up behind her to be part of her present without her consent. She did not turn around to look at her mother; instead, she waited for the woman to walk over to her seat at the table. Which she did when she realized Emma would not turn and confirm her identity.

A flood of emotion went through Emma's body as she saw her mother for the first time in twenty-one years. Like her mother's voice, she looked the same except a little aged. Her heart squeezed and she forced the tears that jumped into her eyes without her consent to be kept at bay. She didn't know why she felt this emotional over seeing this woman. This woman had left; if anything, she should be the one crying. She should be the one emotional.

And she was.

To a degree.

This woman, Clarise, her mother, had short blonde hair with slight grey streaks running through the tresses. She had wrinkles by her eyes, indicating that she smiled a lot. Which made sense, since Emma had heard she had had a family after Emma, a family she could handle, a family she actually wanted. She was dressed sharply for a woman her age - white pantsuit ironed so there were no wrinkles, and a black shirt underneath, offering a nice contrast. She had pink lip stick on her lips and her nails were pink and manicured. Her eyes, unlike Emma's, were blue instead of hazel. She had her father's eyes, a trait she liked. She loved her father's eyes. They were honest and open.

Her mother's right now we're wary but hopeful. Like she wasn't quite sure what to expect.

"Thank you," she said finally in that same strange, familiar voice. "For calling me. For meeting with me."

"I really didn't have a choice," Emma said before she could

stop herself. That sounded harsh, even for her. She pressed her lips together and looked away. "Mom, I'm pregnant."

"Oh." Emma couldn't decipher that word so she didn't try. "Are congratulations in order?"

"Yes, they are," she snapped.

Her mother recoiled slightly. Emma clenched her jaw. She would not let this woman make her feel guilty, even if she did feel it squirm around in the pit of her stomach.

"It wasn't as though I made a mistake," Emma said through gritted teeth, her eyes narrowed as she looked at the woman who looked so much like her it was scary. And unnerving. "A mistake I planned to walk away from."

Her mother gritted her teeth and looked away, and for a second - just a quick second that vanished as quickly as it had come - Emma felt herself flinch internally at what she had just said. But why should she care if she offended her mother? Why should she care about doing anything that might potentially hurt her? What she did to you and to Dad was way worse than a few words aimed to hurt.

Even so, a voice pointed out softly, gently, almost as though it understood where Emma was coming from, but not enough to let her get away with it. *That does not give you the right to be disrespectful. You cannot allow other people to dictate your own behavior. Then you become a victim. And that's the last thing you want to be.*

Emma pressed her lips together. She could admit that the voice was probably correct but that didn't mean that Emma was going to apologize, either. She would just watch what she said from this point on.

"I called you here because I had my first appointment a couple of days ago," Emma began but Clarise jumped in.

"Really?" She seemed genuinely interested. "How did that go?"

Emma had to bite her lip to keep from sharing everything with her mother. She was surprised by the incessant desire to share, but maybe that was because she was excited now, to be a mother, and she wanted to share the news with everyone.

"The baby and I are healthy," Emma said with a nod. "Anyway, the doctor wanted a family history of both of my parents. I thought Dad's would be enough but since I have... access to you and since you can tell me, they insisted I reach out to you to get one. For the baby."

"Oh." Her mother's eyes dropped to the surface of the table. Emma refused to feel sorry for her. Who knew? There was a good chance she was being manipulated. Clarise was good at pretending to care when she obviously didn't. "So you didn't want to reach out yourself?"

"No." Emma did not flinch when she said the word. She did not look away. When her mother picked her eyes up, Emma continued. "You cannot possibly expect me to want to reach out to you when you walked out on me and Dad because it was too hard for you. We survived, Mom. Without you. You were supposed to be there." She immediately stopped herself. The tears sprung up unexpectedly, and she knew if she kept talking, they would fall.

"Oh, honey," she replied, reaching for her daughter's hands, but Emma yanked them away.

Emma wasn't going to allow this woman to touch her, to feel sorry for her. Not after what she did. She didn't want sympathy, she didn't want this woman to feel sorry for herself due to the decisions that she made.

"Please don't," Emma said, trying not to snap at her but wanting to be as firm as she could. Clarise might just see her as a child, as Her child, which meant she might assume that she could tell Emma what to do simply because it was her biological right to do so. The problem was, Emma did not believe biology dictated authority and she wasn't about to let her mom think that either. That might work for her new children, for her new family, but it wasn't going to work for her.

Emma took a breath and locked eyes with her mother. "I'm

only here to get your medical history," she said. Then, in a softer voice, "I'm only here for the baby. I'm not here because I want to have a relationship with you."

Her mother's eyes filled with tears but she kept them at bay. She nodded her head, rubbing her lips together.

"I suppose that's a fair statement," she murmured. "What I did to you and your father -"

"I don't want an apology," Emma said, almost annoyed.

"I wasn't going to give one," she replied, pushing her brows up almost as though to challenge Emma. "What I did... it wasn't right. I'm not going to apologize for it because at the time, I did what I thought was the best thing for me. Does that make it the right thing? Absolutely not. I know that now. But I want to make it right."

"So," Emma said, furrowing her brow, trying to understand her mother through the confusion. "You know you did something wrong but you're not sorry for it?"

"I'm not sorry for anything I do," she said. "That makes me selfish, I know. But it also makes me honest and present. You were... you ARE my first child. And having children after you makes me appreciate just how special the first child is. As I hope you'll realize without making the same mistake I did." She reached out and grabbed Emma's hand, clutching it in her fingers before Emma even had the chance to pull away. "Thank you for being willing to call me even after all I put you through. I am aware that you did so not because of me but because of your unborn child. I'm happy to give you any information you need but..." She paused, rubbing her lips together. "It would make me extremely happy if you would consider allowing me to be part of your life again."

Emma wanted to say no. But she stopped.

'The baby,' a voice pointed out. 'This is for the baby.'

It took everything out of her but she nodded her head. "Fine," she said. "I'll be open to it when that time comes."

Chapter 17

THE GULLS WON both away games and brought back the series to Newport tied. Playoff series were best four out of seven so each team had an opportunity to take the lead. Emma needed it to be Newport. Now that they had arrived at the play-offs, she didn't want them to get out so soon.

They deserved to be there. Kyle, especially, deserved to be there.

He had been on fire the last two games, managing to stay out of the penalty box for the most part, except during one instance where he hooked a Sun player after the guy chopped at his hands. Of course, the ref only picked up on the retaliation so Kyle got the box. This completely pissed off Emma because the Gulls announcers as well as the general announcers for NBC and the NHL Network all said Kyle Underwood had some of the best hands in the league. Every time Emma heard someone say this, she smirked, because he definitely had the best hands she was aware of. But he was a star player and it was the refs' job to call incidental contact on a skill player, especially from a fourth liner like Gobb, who was trying to get Kyle off the ice. Which he did. Kyle shouldn't have to defend himself, though he would without hesitation. Like Alec Schumacher - his line mate - Zachary Ryan, and James Negan, he could definitely handle himself on the ice, even though the Gulls had fighters to defend them.

Kyle was gone four days - two games up in Sacramento, and there was usually a day between games to give the players a rest.

Kyle came back the fourth day and Emma waited for him in the John Wayne Airport baggage pickup. When she saw him, she ran toward him, throwing her arms up and jumping into his arms. He laughed, pulling her close.

She was never like this. She didn't tend to miss him when he was gone, knowing he would come back. But this break, this time away, put things into perspective. He had a game tomorrow night, a game that was incredibly important. If they could win it, they could build confidence going into Game 6.

But for now, that game could wait. Everything else could wait. She wanted to be around him, to feel him touch her and kiss her. To feel him move inside her. To hear him laugh and to hear his stomach rumble with hunger. To hear him softly snore next to her.

"I didn't expect such an affectionate greeting," he murmured in her ear, pulling her close to him even more, somehow balancing his backpack and his luggage while carrying her.

"Should I refrain?" Emma murmured against his throat, her eyes sparkling. This felt nice. This felt good. She was never a big proponent of public displays of affection but Kyle made every- thing... different.

"Never," he told her and she felt her heart clench together with happiness.

They headed straight through the sliding doors without picking up any luggage - the benefits of flying on a private jet - and headed straight for the parking lot. Emma's father had dropped her off here with a backpack and nothing else, which meant Kyle was her ride.

"I probably should have told you before," Emma said with a grin as she let Kyle open the passenger door for her of his sleek silver Mercedes Benz. She slid into the leather seat and clicked on her seatbelt as Kyle sat in his chair. "I planned to spend the night tonight. If that's okay. I know you guys have a day off so I figured it was the perfect time to take advantage of you." She winked.

"I'm not complaining," he told her with a grin before placing his right hand on her thigh.

"I missed you," she told him, her tone genuine. "I'm really proud of how you played, Kyle. You really stepped up. You had the game winner in Game 3. You were on fire." From the corner of her eye, she saw Kyle flush red and didn't actually respond. He hated being complimented due to the discomfort he felt but he never told her not to do it. It did make him feel good after all, and that was her job as his girlfriend. To make him feel good.

"I really stepped up my training," he told her, throwing a glance at her over his shoulder.

"You can tell," she said, nodding with enthusiasm. "But that asshole who chopped your hands totally should have gotten a two-minute."

"You saw that?" he asked with a wry grin.

"Of course I did," she told him. "I know you're a pest but you don't go out of your way to retaliate unless someone did something first."

The drive to his home in a quiet gated community just before PCH was relaxed. The windows were rolled down and the Southern California breeze that seemed a permanent fixture in Newport Beach - especially close to the ocean - was tangling Emma's blonde hair. But she didn't care. It felt good. She was driving through her favorite place in the world with her favorite person in the world.

Well, *two* favorite people in the world.

When they pulled up to Kyle's modern town home - white

paint and a dark roof - they got out of the car. Emma watched him pause in order to breathe in the familiar air and let out a huff of relief at being home. She smiled. She was glad he was home as well.

They walked through the attached garage and into the carpeted hallway that led either to his tiled kitchen on the right or to his living room on the left. Without warning, Kyle tossed Emma over his shoulder and headed left, passing the living room to head to the staircase that led up to the bedrooms.

She squealed, feeling the blood rush to her head as she clutched Kyle's shirt tightly between her fingers. She wasn't sure if it would make a difference, but at least it gave her something to hold onto. She laughed as he led her up the stairs and into his bedroom before placing her gently on the bed.

"I guess with you being pregnant, we don't have to use condoms anymore, do we?" he asked with a small grin on his face.

Emma's mouth dropped. "Did you just make a joke, Kyle Underwood?" she asked, not bothering to hide her surprise. There was a teasing flint in her eye as well, just so he understood she wasn't trying to make fun of him.

"What can I say?" he asked, slowly making his way over to Emma. He hunched down, hopping into the bed and positioning himself over her so he could look over her. Emma felt her heart start to race as she looked up at him with what could only be described as a feral smile. "I'm happy."

"Is that so?" she asked, slowly raising a brow, her lips curled up. "And what has made you happy?"

"You," he murmured before slowly easing his face down so his lips touched hers. "And this baby." Without warning, he slid down so he could place a gentle kiss on her abdomen. Emma didn't understand why but that single kiss set her body on fire.

It wasn't long before he slowly began to strip her free of the clothing she wore on her body. She bit her bottom lip, feeling her hazel eyes turn bronze at the way he was doing it. They had been together for nearly two years. She should be used to this; she should be used to him, but she wasn't. She didn't think she would ever be.

The air squeezed her skin together so goosebumps rippled across her bare skin. Her nipples hardened, especially when Kyle unclasped her bra and gently tugged the straps from her shoulders before tossing it over the side of the bed.

Instantly, his mouth found her nipple and her entire body seized up. She reached for her head, digging her fingers into his scalp to tug him closer to her skin. She loved when his mouth exploded her body, like he was Indiana Jones looking for the holy grail. His hand grabbed hold of her cheek, tilting her head back as though to show that he was the one in charge right now, not her. She whimpered, not because she was pouting, but because she liked it. She could be so controlling in everyday life that when he decided to take charge and dominate her, she was keen to let him have his way with her.

When he finished with one, he moved to the other. He loved teasing her with his teeth, with his tongue, loved the feeling of her squirming underneath him. It was part of the reason why she wanted to take that away, to show he did not make her as weak as he did. But she couldn't help herself.

Without warning, and because she liked to remind him that even though he was on top, she was still in charge, she managed to flip him over so he was on his back and she straddled his hips. He let out a surprised but otherwise pleased grunt and immediately grabbed her hips like he owned them, like they were his. And they were. He helped position her over his cock and eased her over him, impaling him with his hardness.

Emma's eyes clenched shut and she threw her head back. Her mouth dropped open but no sound came out and she furrowed her brow, reveling in the feeling of Kyle stretching her to her core, demanding to be let in, pushing his way through all of her barriers.

When he was finally inside of her, she paused, not moving a

muscle. He looked at her with slitted eyes, waiting for her to take charge. Waiting for her to let him know it was okay for him to move, to really feel her slickness coat him, armor him, drown his cock in her warmth. She felt him twitch in anticipation.

She slowly opened her eyes before looking at him, a feral smile slithering on her face. She could feel her eyes cloud over with lust, and she placed her hands flat on his chest, using him as a way to balance herself. And then, finally, she started to move.

He let out a groan, almost as though he was surprised how it felt, as though they had never had sex the past couple of years. It was a noise that caused her to get goosebumps all over her body and her nipples to harden. Kyle always grabbed them in his big hands, caressing them with his long fingers, almost as though he were trying to warm her up, to soften them, even though he loved looking at them when they were hard. He would see how he could stay away from them, like a dog waiting until his master told him to eat the treat sitting on his nose.

She loved being on top. She knew her body well enough to know exactly the angle to position herself to hit her core perfectly. Her left hand always reached her clit, spreading her lips so she had better access to it. She knew Kyle loved watching her do this, that somehow it got him harder than he already was. And Jesus, it always got her off. His thick cock deep inside her was the perfect accessory to help her do so.

It wasn't long before she shattered around him. He was receptive if her climax, telling her nasty things he reserved for times like this before following into blissful submission. It wasn't long before they both fell asleep.

Chapter 18

EMMA WOKE up to Kyle softly kissing her neck, his hand cupping her still-flat stomach. Before she even opened her eyes, her lips curled into a smile and she felt herself stretching into his kisses.

"I can't believe we created a life that's inside of you right now," he told her in a gentle murmur. "You're still so tiny."

Emma chuckled. "I'll probably be tiny until four or five months," she said, cracking open her eyes so she could look at him. She had never seen him look awed before, like he was simply amazed by her, by the fact that he was going to be a father.

He leaned towards her stomach. "Hey, little guy," he said to her stomach. "You gonna be a hockey player like Daddy? Huh?"

"The baby can't hear until I'm well into my second trimester, possibly the beginning of my third," she said with a grin.

Kyle shrugged. "I don't care," he said. "I'm going to talk to him every day so he gets used to my voice."

Emma felt herself grin. "How do you know the baby is a boy?" she asked him, cocking her head to the side. "My gut feeling say it's a girl and since we know I'm only having one child, we both can't be right."

He shrugged. "Regardless," he said. "The baby will be graceful like Mom and gritty like Dad. And they'll be strong because we both are, in our own ways. Boy or girl, I'm happy. I'm excited. I've started clearing out one of my guest bedrooms to make a nursery."

"Oh, really?" she teased.

He nodded his head and placed a chaste kiss on her lips before trailing downward, caressing her jawline, moving back to the column of her throat. Further down, across her collar bone, towards her breasts. She held her breath, waiting. She loved when he caresses her breasts, took the nipples in his mouth and sucked like they were popsicles on a cold day. Her body twinged, her core dripped with moisture, just thinking about it.

"How did things go with your mother?" he asked her, stopping, just before her nipple. If she arched her back, her nipple would touch his mouth. She was tempted to do it, needed to feel him on her skin, not wanting to talk...

But this wasn't about just her. It was about both of them.

"It went as well as could be expected," she said in a strained voice. "She did tell me what I wanted to know but then she asked..." She sighed, feeling a heap of conflicting feelings swirl around in her chest, squeezing her heart. "She asked if she could be part of my life. Our life." She looked down at Kyle, tucking her chin down so she could lock eyes with him.

He tensed under her touch. "And what did you say?" he asked after a moment of hesitation.

She shrugged. She hated how their intimate moment was ruined by talks of her mother but it wasn't something she could help since Kyle wanted to know.

"I said I'd think about it," she finally replied with a shrug, picking her eyes up to look at Kyle. "As much as I want to blame her for leaving me and my dad - which I do - I'm not going to deny our child a relationship with her grandmother."

His lips quirked up and he cupped her cheek with his large palm and tilted her head black so he could look her in the eye. "That was very mature of you," he told her. That quirked smile slid wider onto his face as his eyes dropped to her stomach. "I can't believe that heartbeat." He shook his head in disbelief, his eyes going back to her stomach. "It was so strong. Like a church bell."

She felt her wrinkle her brow. "That was pretty deep," she said.

He pretended to be offended. "Are you saying I'm not normally deep?" he asked her before placing a kiss just underneath her ear. "I can show you how deep I can go..." He let his voice trail off and placed another kiss on the side of her throat.

She shuddered, her eyes rolling to the back of her head as she let herself feel his caresses, his lips on her most sensitive parts of her skin. He always knew how to touch her in just the right way...

"Yes," she replied. "Please do."

She could feel him smile against her skin, which caused her to smile as well.

He trailed kisses down her chest before slipping over her nipple. She let out a garbled moan, arching her back up in order to get more out of him, to get closer to him. Her hand reached up to clutch the back of his head, her fingers losing themselves in his short blond hair.

God, this felt so good.

How could she have taken him for granted?

When he finished with her right breast, he moved to her left one. More tingles shot up her spine as his left hand trailed down her curves until they reached the apex between her thighs. Without warning, he pushed past her folds and slid a digit into her opening. He grunted through his sucking, feeling how slick and warm and tight she was. She moaned again, tilting her hips up as though she was desperate for more.

And she was.

"Kyle," she gasped out. "Please."

She hated begging. Normally, refused to do it.

But she couldn't help it. Not when he was treating her body like a goddamn canvas and he was painting a picture with his tongue.

"Why are you in such a rush?" he asked her. "We have all the time in the world." He bent his head back down to capture a nipple in his mouth. She gasped, throwing her head back, forgetting whatever it was she was going to tell him.

He slowly slid his digit in and out of her, teasing her. She clenched her muscles around him and he stifled his own groan. She wanted him to think about what it would feel like once his cock was coated with her juices, inside her warmth, snug and suffocating. Judging by his reactions, he was doing just that.

She bit her lip, concealing another groan as he stuck his finger deeper into her.

Jeez, he always knew just how to touch her. She didn't even know how it was possible. All she knew was that he had the best hands in the league - something she could attest to personally. It wasn't long before he had her on bed, writhing, breathing heavily, and begging for release. Kyle did not respond to her pleading; instead, he kept his eyes focused on the task at hand, watching as he slowly inserted his finger inside of her before twisting it and pulling out. He seemed so fascinated by her slickness, by her core, by her body, that she felt as though she was some kind of goddess, a holy thing he worshipped with every ounce of his being. She didn't quite understand it because no one had treated her this way.

'Because you never allowed anyone to treat you this way,' the voice pointed out. 'You always kept your guard up, wary of anyone who wanted to tear it down. Until now, of course.'

Emma pressed her lips together, squeezing her eyes shut. She nearly reached down to take a chunk of Kyle's hair and pull on it just so he would allow her to release the pleasure he had been building up inside of her. It was too much. It was too painful for her to bear any longer.

Almost as though he could read her mind, he pulled out from her. She let out a strangled cry of protest, opening her eyes to glare at him when he was already on top of her, thrusting himself inside of her so quickly Emma barely blinked before she realized what happened.

She let out a groan that was surprised, satisfied, and relieved, all at the same time. Her hands immediately reached for him, her fingers sinking into his flesh. He hissed before nipping at her bottom lip with his teeth, growling at both the pleasure and the pain she was causing him.

"Jesus Christ," he muttered. "I just fucked you yesterday and it still feels like the first goddamn time."

She gripped him tighter, her thighs opening while her ankles locked around his hips, trying to position him deeper. Until -

Oh, yes, that was the spot.

Her eyes rolled to the back of her head and she moaned, loosening her grip on him because she couldn't hold on. Didn't have the strength to release him but she couldn't get a grip - not when it felt so good.

"Kyle," she managed to get out. She couldn't formulate anything beyond that, however. Instead, she found his scalp again.

"That's right, baby," he murmured, his voice filled with longing. She loved when he talked dirty to her. "Fuck, I can feel you getting even wetter. Jesus, if you don't cum, I'm going to, so you better hurry up and take what's yours."

And there it was - her undoing. Her heart echoed through her head - the only sound she could hear - as she felt herself step off the precipice and fall into a world of pleasure.

He followed shortly after but she barely noticed. She was lost in her world, feeling her body twitch and convulse. Her arms were limp like boiled noodles, her head was high in the sky, among the cloud.

When they finally finished, his head collapsed in her shoulder. He was careful not to place all of his weight on her, especially now that she was carrying his child, but he always liked to be close to her enough to breathe in the scent of her skin, to taste the sweat off her shoulder.

Emma found it within her to wrap her arms around him, but it was difficult being so exhausted. She could barely keep her eyes open as she felt him nuzzle her neck, coil his arms around her waist and hold onto her possessively.

"I am so in love with you," he murmured into her shoulder.

Her lips curled up into a smile and she began to trace mindless patterns into his skin. She felt him shudder underneath his touch and smiled. It was still amazing to her, the sort of power she had over this strong hockey player. How she could bring him to his knees.

"It feels so good to finally fuck you without a condom on," he continued. "I know it's crass, but coming inside of you feels like home."

Emma snorted. "That was crass," she agreed, "but also romantic."

"Will you be there tonight?" he asked. He sounded so young, so vulnerable, asking her this question. He didn't look at her, keeping his eyes away from hers so she wouldn't be able to read them, so she wouldn't be able to see how much it meant to him that she was there and why it was so important that she was. He couldn't do this without her.

Well, technically he could. She knew he could. But there was something different with her. And Emma had been withholding herself from it, afraid it would disappear as soon as it was here. Like sand slipping through her fingers.

"Of course," she told him, running her fingers gently through his blond hair. "I'm always going to be there. Except when I'm giving birth, obviously."

He chuckled, his hand sliding from her hip to her stomach. "I've wanted to marry you six months into our relationship, you know. I'm pretty sure you weren't pregnant at that point."

Emma felt herself smile. "Why are you telling me this?" she asked.

"Because I'm hoping you'll reconsider my offer and marry me," he replied.

Emma shook her head. "No," she told him. "You do not get to ask me to marry you right after good sex. How am I supposed to know the hormones aren't talking and not you."

"Fine," he said. "I'll ask when I'm not being tempted by sleep due to an amazing fuck. I do owe you another dinner at Dimitri's restaurant. The chicken yoki soup is delicious, you have to try it."

Emma chuckled and shook her head. "Fine," she said, "but you need to focus on hockey and I need to figure out this whole thing with my mom, dancing, and deciding whether or not to say yes." Kyle's head snapped up and she grinned. "Just kidding." He placed his head back on her shoulder, seemingly placated. "For now, let's just enjoy this moment. There's no where I'd rather be than with you. Both of you."

And she meant it.

Want to know when Book 5 comes out?

Rumors & Roughing: Book 5 in the Slapshot Series will be released October 27, 2017. Preorder it now for 99 pennies - but only for a limited time!

Want updates on when my latest book comes out, exclusive giveaways, and free stuff? Sign up for my newsletter here!

Did You Like Positives & Penalties?

As an author, the best thing a reader can do is leave an honest review. I love gathering feedback because it shows me you care and it helps me be a better writer. If you have the time, I'd greatly appreciate any feedback you can give me. Thank you!

Acknowledgments

The Anaheim Ducks because they're my team no matter what - especially the team from 2011. My inaugural season. ;)

My family

My friends

The work squad

Susan H., Cindy F., Angi, and Summer for your amazing edits and suggestions! My writing is better because of you!

Susanna Lynn, for your beautiful cover. It's amazing and stunning and perfect!

Thank you to my readers who have fallen in love with this series, with hockey, and with the amazing players. I write for YOU!

Frank & Kylee, Josh & Jacob, for your continued love, support, and understanding

Also by Heather C. Myers

The Slapshot Series: A Sports Romance

Blood on the Rocks, Snapshot Prequel, Book 1 Her grandfather's murdered and she's suddenly thrust with the responsibility of owning and managing a national hockey team. That, and she decides to solve the murder herself.

Grace on the Rocks, **Slapshot Prequel, Book 2** A chance encounter at the beach causes sparks to fly...

Charm on the Rocks, **Slapshot Prequel Book 3** When you know it's wrong but it feels so right

The Slapshot Prequel Box Set

Exes & Goals, Book 1 of the Slapshot Series Most people have no regrets. She has one.

Black Eyes & Blue Lines, **Book 2 of the Slapshot Series** He drives her crazy - and not in a good way. But she can't get him out of her head.

Lip Locks & Blocked Shots, **Book 3 of the Slapshot Series** He's the last person she should fall in love with and the only one that ever stood a chance.

Positives & Penalties, **Book 4 of The Slapshot Series** One gorgeous hockey player plus one night of passion equals two pink lines...

Also by Heather C. Myers

Modern Jane Austen Retellings

Denial Matchmaking is supposed to be easy. But Madeline is going to learn that love can't be planned when she starts to fall for the last person she ever thought she would, who also happens to be the man her best friend claims to love as well.

Stubborn Marion is a die-hard USC fan. Aiden goes to UCLA Law School. If only college rivalries were the worst of their problems. They say opposites attract. Well, some crash into each other.

Also by Heather C. Myers

New Adult Contemporary Romance

Save the Date As daughter of a man in charge of the CIA, Gemma knew her father was overprotective. She just never thought he would assign a man she couldn't stand to be her bodyguard under the rouse of a fake marriage.

On Tour with the Rockstar Holly Dunn didn't know that when she began studying at a rock concert, the lead singer would call her out on it. Tommy Stark didn't know he'd be intrigued by her odd sort of ways, which was why hew invited her to go on tour with him.

Foolish Games She was everything he didn't want in a woman and everything he couldn't resist. She thought he was arrogant on top of other things.

Falling Over You She wasn't supposed to see him, hear him, or feel him because he was dead - a ghost. She wasn't supposed to fall in love with him because she was engaged.

Hollywood Snowfall It's getting cold in Hollywood, so cold, there's a good chance the City of Angels will finally get snow.

Also by Heather C. Myers

Dark Romance

A Beauty Dark & Deadly He's the most beautiful monster she's even seen

A Reputation Dark & Deadly Logan Jeffrey has a reputation

Also by Heather C. Myers

Young Adult Novels

<u>Trainwreck</u> Detention is not the place where you're supposed to meet your next boyfriend, especially when he's Asher Boyd, known pothead and occasional criminal. But he makes good girl Sadie Brown feel something she hasn't really felt before - extraordinary.

Also by Heather C. Myers

Science Fiction/Fantasy

Battlefield Just because they were, quite literally, made for each other didn't mean they had to actually get along.

Made in United States
Orlando, FL
22 March 2024

45046925R00078